Kid Dakota

and the

Secret at Grandma's House

Walt Heyer

Copyright © 2015 by Walt Heyer

Kid Dakota and the Secret at Grandma's House
By Walt Heyer

Printed in the United States of America
ISBN: 978-1508465218

All rights reserved solely by the author. The author guarantees all contents are original and do not infringe on the legal rights of any other person or work. No part of this book may be reproduced in any form without the permission of the author. The views expressed in this book are not necessarily those of the publisher.

Contact the author:
Kid.Dakota@yahoo.com

Website:
www.KidDakotaBook.com

ONE

The Beginning

Grandpa and Nana roll into L.A.

The warm sun was slowly setting over the west coast of California in the summer of 1944 in the fast growing city of Los Angeles, which because of its earthquakes, is often called "Shaky Town." Even in the 1940s, this was a sprawling city with a split personality. On one side of the city you could find the uber rich with all their glitz and glamor. The streets were framed with majestic eighty-foot palm trees gently swaying with the ocean breeze, giving the impression of dancing. People were so rich a hundred dollar bill was often just tip money. The streets were filled with the opulence of Rolls Royce or Bentley eye candy slowly rolling past. The men shopping on Rodeo Drive stepped lively along the tidy sidewalks in their expensive A. Testoni Norvegese shoes. You could even catch a glimpse of a movie star casually walking past you in front of the Gucci, Giorgio Armani and Ralph Lauren stores. Dream, baby, dream.

The other side of the city's split personality was not far away, just a twenty minute drive. The city was divided by a street known by the locals as "Fig." This street cut through the heart of Shaky Town and stretched for miles south toward the harbor cities and north to the hills. No majestic palm-tree-lined streets on the north; no Bentley automobiles roll past. On this side of the city where the working families lived you were more likely to catch a glimpse of an old broken-down Chevy hooked to the back of a tow truck. This blue collar working class neighborhood built in the 1920s featured no glitz or glamor, just old cars, old homes and old people. In this part of L.A. called Highland Park a hundred dollars was two weeks' pay.

Tucked behind a junkyard fence in Highland Park was a little house, the home of Nana and one-legged Grandpa Mike Austin. Kid Dakota often stayed for the weekend in their care while his parents went camping or fishing.

Grandpa and Nana Austin had rolled into L.A. on a cloud of old Texas dust. They followed the course set by their only daughter, Ellie, who moved to L.A. for work and soon after married Chuck Martin. The Austins were poor folks with limited education. All that book smart stuff had eluded this Texas family. Grandpa and Nana Austin thought they were lucky to find this shack of a home on "Fig" by the tow yard. Even young Kid Dakota wasn't so sure how lucky they were. The little house needed paint some twenty years ago. It was a rundown old home, but it was their home. No landscaping here; just dirt surrounded by a rusty chain link fence "decorated" on top with barbed wire. This was called the front yard. The place was flanked on both sides by old pepper trees standing wide and tall providing some real good shade during the heat of the summer. But the big trees consistently shed their old dry leaves, causing a mess no one ever cleaned up.

This little one bedroom house was built as part of the wrecking yard to house the caretakers. Mike Austin was, in fact, the tow truck driver and caretaker of the wrecking yard, and was provided this as a free place to live. Grandpa Mike drove the tow truck and used his artificial leg to push the clutch pedal down to disengage the clutch to shift the gears. The people with whom Grandpa worked nicknamed him "Stumpy." People were sometimes harsh when trying to be funny, Dakota thought. The people who joked around calling him "Stumpy" didn't know the amputated leg gave Grandpa Mike fits of pain much of the time. Pushing the clutch caused blisters on his leg stump.

Dakota had never asked Grandpa about his leg. It just didn't feel right to ask, but one night there came that special moment. Grandpa was removing his artificial leg in front of Dakota. Dakota looked on, horrified, standing only three feet from Grandpa. Dakota was stunned because he had never seen how ugly the leg stump was; the end of it was full of sores. Grandpa's face grimaced with pain.

Dakota, slowly, in a scared, soft voice, got up the courage to ask, "Grandpa, how did your leg get like that?" Grandpa Mike managed a rare smile, no doubt tickled by his young grandson's inquisitive interest. Grandpa's smile faded as he sat there, his stump exposed. "You're a young boy. I tell ya this, if a man wants you to know about his wooden leg, he's gonna tell ya. No need to ask him. But I'll tell ya this once."

Grandpa Mike's tone toward the young boy sounded like a stern warning, "Jumpin' on a moving freight train ain't no good. Real dumb it was." Dakota remained silent as Grandpa continued, "There just weren't much for a teen kid to do fer fun in the 1880s and 1890s. Climbin' on freight trains, ridin' a bit, then jumpin' off was a game we played."

The youngster sat mesmerized on the floor listening. This was special. Grandpa never said anything about his stump leg. Dakota remained silent as Grandpa went on to tell the story. This grandson was listening to every word.

Grandpa started spilling his guts, "That day the dadgum rain was a fallin' hard. I was walkin' the train tracks. I listened; off in the distance a train horn was blowin'." Grandpa Mike wasn't making eye contact with the young boy, rather he looked into the distance at the memory as he continued the story, "That train horn was a blowin' and I wanted to jump that train. That's it. Just jump on; ride a bit, then jump off."

Young Dakota noticed a tear falling down Grandpa Mike's cheek. The pain of the story forced Grandpa to turn his head away to hide the tears. Grandpa quickly continued with the story, "I see that train; it was a comin' on toward me, travelin' fast." The young kid was looking at Grandpa, all still, like he was holding his breath. You could have heard the sound of dust settling, it was so quiet.

Grandpa Mike continued, "I looked up. There she was; that train makin' a big noise: the wheels, the horn, the engine. It was movin' fast." Taking a deep breath, Grandpa struggled to complete his old story, "I was a runnin' fast alongside that train;

the rain a fallin'. I grabbed that wet cold steel ladder on the side of the train. I yanked myself up and put my foot on the steel step just like I always did." Dakota, gripped by the story, said, "You really ran fast, Grandpa Mike." Grandpa Mike shook his head side to side looking down at the floor, "Fast as an 18-year old could, but not so smart. The steel step was wet and slick. My foot come off the step and down I went, under the train. The big train wheels rolled over my leg; cut it off like it was nothin'."

Silence. Neither grandson nor grandpa spoke. Without another word Grandpa Mike rubbed some ointment on the stump sores and placed his artificial leg brace on. Then Grandpa stood up, pulled his pant leg down over that man-made leg and with his stiff limp walked out the front door. The last sound Dakota heard was the screen door slamming.

Kid Dakota knew Grandpa would never tell that story again and there would be no more questions from his grandson either. He had all he needed to know.

Nana was short, plump and unkempt, a dirt poor crippled ole' Texan who walked with a waddle. Most profound was her flower-patterned apron that held a half pint of whiskey in a sagging pocket. She cut an unforgettable picture as she sat for hours slowly rocking back and forth in the wood rocker with a cigarette dangling from her lips, the crochet needle in her hand swiftly moving yarn.

This little home was where on many weekends you would find Kid Dakota staying. While his parents went fishing or camping, Dakota was assigned to stay with Nana and Grandpa Mike, his mother's parents. Grandpa Mike was either off driving the tow truck or just sitting very quietly in the front room, hardly ever saying a word, waiting for the next call to tow a broken-down or wrecked automobile. Nana loved her whiskey, keeping that whiskey bottle within arm's reach. The small and skinny four-year-old Dakota fit right in. His hair was often disheveled, just a ball-playing kid. Like most boys he knew, he was most comfortable when sporting torn and tattered dirty jeans and his scuffed-up, brown high-top shoes.

Los Angeles in the mid 1940s was no easy time for anyone, especially not for the poor folks from rural Texas. At least they were living in a house, even if it was behind a bunch of old wrecked cars in Highland Park. The L.A. area was like a magnet because of the idyllic weather and the closeness of the Pacific Ocean. If you had ever been to the beach there, it would come as no surprise that three million people lived in L.A. prior to 1940 and one million more made L.A. home by the end of the 1940s.

Dakota's mother, Ellie, had pulled herself out from under her fractured, dirt-poor childhood having barely survived in a small Texas town to be a working girl in L.A. The attractive teenager caught the eye of a friendly young salesman, Chuck Martin, who called on the company where she worked. Before long, they fell in love and married. She was only seventeen.

Things got much better for Ellie when she married Chuck. Chuck Martin was six years older than Ellie. He was successful in his career as an industrial salesman and earned an above average income. Chuck was the traveling salesman everybody loved, the kind of man with whom people just wanted to sit and talk because they felt better whenever he was around.

Ellie married a smart, hard-working guy in Chuck Martin. She soon gave birth to their first child, Danny. Then eighteen months later, Dakota was born. At the age of twenty, Ellie was the mother of two boys.

Dakota was just one small part of two very different families: one, his mom's parents, the down-home Texas folks, and the other, his papa's parents, transplants from Chicago, who were quite the opposite of the Texas bunch. You might have said Mom Ellie married up.

Papa's father, Clint Martin, was a businessman and lay pastor, and smart. He started L.A.'s first department store and ran it successfully. He was a short guy who loved the outdoors, especially camping and fishing. Papa's mother, Flossie Martin, came from a strict puritan religious family. Flossie was tough but she had a soft side. Years after she had raised her own children, Flossie talked her husband Clint into adopting her sister's illegitimate baby, Kyle, to cover up the family scandal when her sister became pregnant from an affair with an American Indian boy.

Two families. Two very different upbringings.

Dakota was raised in a time of turmoil but also it was a time when people didn't give up. They never gave up during the war, patriotically fighting the world's enemies. This perseverance was hard-wired into Dakota. It was the way everyone looked at life—never giving up, no matter how difficult the battle.

The 1940s were a pivotal and historical time in U.S. history. An ugly world war was raging across Europe. The war kicked off in 1939 becoming the most widespread war in history, with more than 100 million people from 30 different countries serving in military units. Countries were in a state of total war. The major participants threw their entire economic, industrial, and scientific capabilities behind the war effort, erasing any distinction between civilian manufacturing and military resources.

The production of U.S. automobiles was halted from 1942 to 1945 to keep up with the demands of war materials. The auto industry transformed itself to manufacture tanks, trucks, jeeps, airplanes, bombs, torpedoes, steel helmets and ammunition in their effort to serve the needs of our country by keeping supplies flowing to our military men. It was truly like no other time.

The total commitment to war also produced very resilient, self-reliant, God-filled men and women during a time when family and moral values were everything. People kept their problems to themselves. Families during this time didn't cope by popping anti-depressants or sitting with the psychotherapist. Individuals looked to themselves and remained optimistic, whatever problems they had.

Families enjoyed the sounds of music, songs and dancing as a means of diversion and inspiration through hard times. Real men, real muscle, and real hard work identified the generation of the 1940s. Music filled every room of every home during the 1940s: sounds like classic pop, big band sounds, swing and a new generation of big voices known as the crooners emerged, Frank Sinatra and the like. During this era you could listen to rhythm and blues, country and western, even folk music. Just down from Grandpa Mike's on old Fig Street was a big music store that sold musical instruments and records. Older brother Danny purchased his first clarinet there.

It didn't make a difference, rich or poor; everyone was listening to the sounds of music.

Some of the popular music was the heart-pounding, flag-waving inspirational sounds of American march music—pure, genuine morale boosters for U.S. citizens and military around the world. Kid Dakota was an active participant. Pumping up the volume on the record player or radio, Dakota would march around the house, stomping his little feet as if he were a uniformed military man. In the living room he paraded to the music he loved, American march music. This little kid also loved to smile and the sound of music made him smile.

During the first five years of Dakota's life, the war raged as people died for freedom from tyrants and evil, and people prayed for the war to end. Prayers were answered, not soon enough for some but, thankfully, by 1945 the war ended and the men started returning home. By some reports fifteen million U.S. military men were being discharged. Not all the military men were returning to the home towns they had left. They were off in every direction across the country. Many located in the sprawling areas of Los Angeles, California.

Just like Mom Ellie's parents, the Austins, had discovered a few years previously, L. A. offered many new opportunities to the returning GIs as these young men looked to renew their lives. Now they were settling far from the battlegrounds and the small hometowns that had limited opportunities for jobs or lacked the warm climate of California. As the population of Los Angeles swelled, housing for all the new residents became a problem to solve.

One afternoon as Dakota rode in the back seat of Papa's green 1941 Ford, he could see the housing boom in L.A. unfolding in front of him as they rode through the wide open spaces of Griffith Park. Car window rolled down, wind in his face, Dakota saw workers building structures. Once open fields of grass were now covered with funny looking structures. Dakota, curious, leaned forward to ask his papa: "Papa, what are those funny-looking buildings out there?" Papa answered, "Little buddy, those little houses are called Quonset huts." Dakota still puzzled, persisted, "Papa, they don't look like any house I ever saw." Papa explained, "The Navy came up with the design. They are building them quickly for the military men and women coming home from the war. They aren't meant to be permanent homes like ours; just a temporary home so the servicemen have somewhere to live until they can find a house like ours. Your mother and I know some people who are going to be living in one of these huts."

Then older brother Danny, a prolific reader, had to get his two cents in on this because he had read about the Quonset huts. Danny, Dakota's smarty pants older brother, was sitting next to Dakota in the car. Showing up his little brother was one of Danny's favorite past-times. He turned his head to look directly at Dakota and said, "Dakota, the shape is a half dome and it's simple to build. The huts will protect the people from the rain." Dakota thought, "How stupid. You don't need to read a book to learn that. You can see that by looking at them." But Dakota kept his mouth shut.

Los Angeles was undergoing big changes and the Quonset huts popping up in Griffith Park were just the start. Everywhere you looked the population was growing, segregated by ethnic group: whites in the west neighborhoods, blacks and Hispanics to the east and south of town center. Japanese-Americans were returning from the internment camps and assimilating into areas of L.A. as well. New churches were opening in vacant buildings all across town.

The war touched every single life in some small or big way. These were the amazing 1940s; forever etched in U.S. history.

No Quonset hut for the Chuck Martin family. They lived in a nice 1,210 square foot house built in 1926. The white stucco home with dark green trim stood tall and proud on the side of a hill located only seven miles north of Los Angeles. Kid Dakota's home was sandwiched in an area of L.A. between Pasadena and Glendale. Glendale was a major shopping area with Sears Roebuck, J. C. Penny and other stores serving the growing bedroom communities. This home was also located near Nana and Grandpa Austin.

Dakota's life story was one of the wildest roller-coaster thrill rides any kid ever had. The events started in nearby Highland Park area of Los Angeles in 1944, where Dakota at age four stayed overnight all too frequently at Nana's house, where his own private war began and the secret that wouldn't let go of the young boy's thoughts took root.

The early world of Dakota was squarely in the hands of Nana.

TWO

Nana's House

Danny and Dakota; Papa and Mom

It was the summer of 1945. Dakota's mom and dad and the boys were standing in the family's kitchen when Papa with a big smile announced, "Hey boys, your mom and I are going away for the weekend. Danny, you'll stay with Grandpa Clint and Grandma Flossie. Dakota, you'll stay with Nana and Grandpa Mike for the weekend." Papa in a louder, drill sergeant voice gave the orders, "Get going and get your clothes, toothbrush, night clothes and some toys to play with. Okay?" As if Papa was asking a question. The boys knew there were no questions; just orders to get moving.

Danny was happy because Papa's father, Grandpa Clint, had a nice collection of balsa wood model airplane kits, glue and all the stuff to build airplanes. Anticipating a weekend of fun, Danny quickly got his stuff in a sack and out the door he went, almost running the short distance to Grandpa Clint's house.

Dakota dropped his head and slowly walked to his bedroom, obviously unhappy. He shoved the clothes he would need in the same old paper bag he always used. Papa looked at Dakota's reluctance and ordered him in a loud voice, "Come on. Let's get going." Seeing Dakota with the paper bag pressed to his chest, Papa grabbed the boy's free hand and walked him out the door. Hand-in-hand with his youngest son, Papa briskly pulled him down the front steps and headed toward the family's green '41 Ford sedan parked on the street in front of the house.

At the bottom of the steps near the car, Dakota, longing to go with Danny, turned his head to catch a glimpse of his brother but Danny was gone, out of sight. Papa opened the back door and loaded Dakota into the back seat of the Ford. It was a typical warm summer afternoon. Dakota wasn't excited about this weekend and didn't want to go, at least not to Nana's.

Papa was a fit man in his late twenties, about 180 pounds and nearly six feet tall. He wore a fedora hat and striped short-sleeved muscle "T" shirt, always with a pack of Chesterfield smokes tucked under his left sleeve at his shoulder. He was the picture of '40s cool.

Papa fired up the old Ford and off they went on the six mile drive to Nana and Grandpa Mike's. The first turn was onto York Boulevard, then about three miles and a right turn onto Avenue

50. Avenue 50 was a familiar winding road Dakota had taken many times traveling to Nana's. Not much to look at from the back seat except old homes. Dakota was looking at the same old gas stations, stores and houses he always saw. Soon they crossed Fig Street. Just beyond the intersection and down the block, Papa turned left at the alley. Only another 70 yards to go and they would arrive at the entrance to the driveway that ran along Nana's side yard.

During that six mile drive not a word had been spoken between Dakota and Papa. Dakota's silence was his way of showing Papa he wasn't happy. Dakota didn't like going to Nana's house. There were no kids to play with, not even his brother. He just felt alone when he was there. It was during these lonely times that Dakota turned to his imaginary friend, Coach, for company. Their method of communication existed purely in Dakota's head, by exchanging thoughts back and forth. Today Dakota needed to talk to someone, so he called on Coach. "I'm not going to be happy staying at Nana's, you know," Dakota thought silently. Coach simply replied, "You have no choice; just do your best to enjoy it." Dakota huffed and puffed a little as if he wanted to blow Nana's house down. He wasn't happy. The response from Coach "to enjoy it" prompted Dakota to try to paste a phony smile on his four-year-old face. Papa brought the Ford to a stop, reached for the door handle and opened it. All the kid could think was, "Papa will get his weekend away while I'm stuck at Nana's again."

Papa could tell Dakota wasn't happy. He started talking to Dakota as they were walking to the front door, "Son, I'll pick you up Sunday afternoon and we'll get your brother and go have a mile-high ice cream cone." The offer of ice cream was Papa's way to cool him off, if only a little. Dakota still wasn't happy. The thought of ice cream on Sunday wasn't much help for this kid. But instead he said, "That sounds good, Papa."

Walking hand-in-hand with Papa along the path to the front door, Dakota looked out of the corner of his eye through the holes of the fence at the wrecked cars in the adjacent wrecking yard. Turning his head the other way he saw their destination, the old shack. Unhappy with either view, he looked up at the big pepper trees, their branches like giant arms big enough to gobble up the little house. The thought made him smile. Dakota needed a smile that would last through two nights at Nana's. Not easy to come by when you don't want to be there.

The warm late afternoon summer sun shined a beam of light directly on the weather-worn front porch. Papa and Dakota climbed up the steps onto the front porch. Dakota saw Nana inside, one fat arm stretched out holding the broken screen door open for the two of them. "Hi, come on in, you two." Once they got past her, Nana waddled on her stocky legs toward her old rocker. As she turned to sit down, Dakota had a full view of her substantial width and her smock apron. The apron looked as if someone had dumped hot ashes down the front. Dakota saw the telltale traces of cigarette burns starting just below her chin all the way down to the pocket where her whiskey bottle was ready for a quick draw up to her lips. Dakota wanted to laugh because it was so funny, like a cartoon, but he politely said nothing and laughed on the inside. Nana wanted Dakota to come over and kiss her but the kid hated the smell of her breath, a combination of smoking and whiskey. It was more like the smell of an old combat boot, he thought.

That Texas gal was some picture. It was difficult not to stare at her. Smoke curled upward through her thinning hair as a cigarette dangled precariously from her lips and threatened to drop more burning ash on the apron below. The rutted well-worn skin on her face covered up the youngish woman she really was. With wire-rimmed glasses at the end of her nose, she wasn't a pretty woman. Her face held the evidence that Texas life had been very hard on her.

She sat her stocky body down. Then she told Dakota, "Now go put your bag on the back porch. Y'always sleep out there in the summer, ya know." Dakota answered, "Okay, Nana." When Dakota returned from the back porch, Papa gave him a hug, said his goodbyes and he was gone. Dakota looked out the window and saw Papa in his green Ford vanish down the alley out of sight. Dakota wished Papa would turn around and come back and take him away from Nana's.

Nana drank too much and crocheted or knitted all day. Dakota watched her pause from time to time from knitting to reach down into the apron pocket. Out of the pocket, up to her lips with one smooth motion, came the flat whiskey bottle. With her free hand, she removed the cigarette from her lips to take a nip of booze. She always called it a nip. Dakota's mom, Ellie, explained that Nana's whiskey was needed for medicinal purpose. Dakota thought she needed a lot of that medicine, that's for sure.

Ellie entrusted her four-year-old boy with Nana even though Nana's record of how she raised Ellie wouldn't have received rave reviews. But with a few nips of whiskey Nana relaxed and seemed harmless enough, even playful. But Nana had some strange ideas for games for her grandson. Dakota was one fun-loving, energetic kid with a fertile and active mind that soaked up everything and everyone around him.

Nana welcomed her weekend charge with the promise of a delicious dinner, "Dakota, when Grandpa gets home, I'll make us some black-eyed peas, along with good ol' chicken and dumplin's and buttermilk to wash it down." Nana loved to cook with thick buttermilk. Nana said, "Everything tastes better with buttermilk."

Dakota wandered out to the back porch, a screened-in room attached to the back of the house. He continued out the door into the yard just to get out of the house. No grass; just dirt all around. This wasn't a fun place for a kid to spend a weekend away from home. The kid walked toward one of the big pepper trees and sat down on the ground. He sat under the tree, sheltered from the sun, outside away from Nana.

Dakota didn't like being in the little house. Dakota liked being off by himself when he visited Nana's. He made a game out of listening to sounds far and near. To Dakota all the sounds were like words telling a story he couldn't see. This young boy was trying to understand where he as a kid fit in the big world of sounds that filled his ears. Sometimes, he liked being quiet because it made him feel invisible and safe.

Just then Dakota heard the familiar sound of Grandpa Mike making his way up the dirt path from the alley to the house. Grandpa Mike limped along on his wooden leg, which kicked up dirt as he scuffed along toward the front porch. Kid Dakota knew Nana would have dinner on the table soon. So Dakota disconnected from his private world of listening to sounds, got up and brushed off his pants. That pepper tree dropped lots of stuff on the ground and sitting under the tree guaranteed a mess on the backside of his pants.

As Dakota pulled opened the front screen door and walked in to greet Grandpa Mike, the kid, for some reason, felt small in a big world. "Hi, Grandpa Mike," he said. "Stumpy" responded in a tired voice, "Hi, Dakota." The kid could hear Nana give a command from the kitchen, "Go, wash up and sit at the table. Dinner's ready. Now go get cleaned up."

Nana was standing over her narrow four-burner white porcelain stove, cooking away. Reaching for a bowl and a big spoon she started dishing up dumplings, chicken and gravy. Nana's Texas style of serving was to blend all the food into one big bowl. The table was already set with corn bread, melted butter and jam. The corn bread was cooked in an iron pan so that it baked into shapes like half a corn cob. There were gravy fixin's in a serving bowl; no one would go hungry tonight. This kid never lacked for a big plate of food at Nana's. She was a darn good cook.

After eating, Dakota popped up from the table like always, going for a ringside spot on the floor in front of the radio. The three were soon gathered around the three-foot-high and two-foot-wide art deco style 1930s Philco radio. No television, but there was a wide variety of radio comedy programs such as *The Great Gildersleeve*, and *Fibber_McGee and Molly*, both big hits back then. Other popular radio programs included *Inner Sanctum Mysteries* with its signature opening and ending sound: an eerie squeaking door that gave Kid Dakota chills.

Classic commercials in the 1940s included Philip Morris, Lucky Strike and Chesterfield cigarettes. Chesterfield ads featured Bob Hope and Ronald Reagan. Philip Morris used an iconic bellhop and their jingle, "Call for Philip Morris." Commercials and news from the war were the only interruptions to the radio shows.

Four-year-old Dakota sat on the dirty rug quietly listening to the shows on the radio, unaware it was becoming his personal teaching tool for learning how to listen and developing his imagination to see the scenes painted by the words. The evenings at Nana's always went this way, with the three of them in the front room listening to the radio: Dakota on the floor in front of the radio, Nana in her old rocker, and Grandpa Mike off in the corner in a chair by himself. Grandpa Mike didn't like to talk much.

No doubt some of the war news that came across the radio waves was scary. For Kid Dakota hearing about the number of soldiers that died was scary. Dakota got a yucky feeling in his stomach whenever deaths were reported. Even in prayer when his mom prayed the nightly prayer to her boys, "Now I lay me down to sleep. I pray the Lord my soul to take. If I should die before I wake, I pray the Lord my soul to take," the part about dying scared Dakota and he often stayed awake trying to grasp what death was.

After listening to their favorite radio shows that night Nana said in a stern voice, "Dakota, it's 9:30 and bedtime; so get ready. The bed's made up for ya." He didn't like arguments so he compliantly said, "Okay." Dakota cleaned up and went to the screened-in back porch where his bed was ready. Dakota didn't like the back porch because of the flies, lots of flies. Nana used these things called "fly ribbons," strips of golden yellow sticky paper about eighteen inches long and two inches wide that dangled from the ceiling. When the flies landed on the paper, they stuck there. The dangling yellow fly ribbons filled with dead black flies were an ugly site. Dakota felt surrounded by them. It sure wasn't something he wanted to see.

Privacy was limited on the back porch—just canvas fabric shades covered the screen walls. The multi-colored striped canvas shades were easy to roll down at night and back up in the day. Quickly, Kid Dakota was snug in bed, using a bundle of towels as a makeshift pillow for his head. His bed was pressed close to a fruit storage bin so that his head almost touched the onions, grapefruit and apples stored there. Over the fruit storage bin Nana had draped her nylon stockings to dry; at least that's what she did that night. Dakota thought this was Nana's way to see if he could resist touching them.

Dakota couldn't resist. He reached his hand out from under the covers to grasp a feel of the silky soft nylon. Dakota thought these stockings could be the same ones Nana had placed over his legs on previous weekend stay overs. But Dakota wondered why they were hanging so close to his bed and draped over onions, grapefruit and apples. They hadn't ever been there before.

Just then Nana entered the back porch, "Dakota, ya like the feel of the nylon stockings, don't ya?" Dakota, with a sheepish smile, said "Yeah, I guess. They're soft and they make me tingle." Telling Nana this made his face glow red. Nana quietly said, "Go ta sleep. We'll see about the nylons tomorrow." She kissed her grandson on the forehead. "Sleep tight, Dakota." The smell of her breath was a mixture of liquor, cigarettes and onions. Dakota's eyes smarted from her breath. It was horrible.

Dakota did like the feel of nylon stockings. He learned how the nylon felt from Nana. Nana routinely dressed this young boy, her little grandson, Dakota, in her female clothes. But she only dressed him this way when no one else was there, just her and her grandson.

Nana's habit of dressing him up started a long time ago. It started as a game. She dressed Dakota with a big smile, "We're gonna play a dress-up game. You'll love it. It'll be fun." Dakota thought it was fun at first. "Dakota, I'll dress you up ta look like a girl." She also told Dakota over and over, "I really like ya as a lil' girl. You make a real nice girl 'cause you're small." Nana was planting, cultivating and nurturing a seed in Dakota's fertile mind that would take root and grow beyond the game and become real.

That night, after the smell of whiskey and cigarettes faded from the room, Dakota laid there awake. He was puzzled and started talking to his imaginary buddy, Coach.

"Coach, why did Nana start playing the dress-up game anyway?"

Coach only said, "I'm not sure it's good for you."

Dakota asked, "If it's bad, why would she do it?"

Coach replied, "It started as a fun game."

Dakota said, "Nana doesn't want me to tell anyone about it."

Coach replied, "You know Papa says if something's a secret, there must be something wrong with it."

Dakota kept sharing his concerns with his buddy, "I don't know. Sometimes, I like the game because it feels good. Nana has fun dressing me up and she always tells me how good I look in her clothes. She never tells me how good I look good as a boy."

Coach, "You'll be up all night thinking about this. Go to sleep."

This confused youngster finally fell off to sleep that night without getting answers to his questions.

The early morning glow of sunrise was lighting up the back porch as Dakota peeked out from his half-opened eyes. From the backyard chicken coop the rooster made his morning announcement: "A new day has been born; now get up!" This was the only house around with chickens in the yard. Nana and Grandpa Mike had come from Texas. They always had fresh eggs for breakfast and chickens for dinner. This family had the 1940s version of fast food: the backyard chicken coop. Dakota learned to be careful where he stepped. There was chicken poop in the chicken coop. He had to dodge it when he went for eggs.

The kid was hungry for breakfast today. Nana told her half-awake grandson, "Wash up now. We're fixin' deep fried donuts to eat with our eggs." Dakota loved donuts and replied eagerly, "Okay, Nana, I'll wash up." After he washed up, the little guy pushed a wooden chair across the room to the stove so he could get up on it and have a good view to watch Nana. She explained to her grandson what she was doing, "I pour oil inta this pan ratch here and turn on the gas burner." Kid Dakota said, "It seems like it is taking forever to get the oil hot, Nana." The kid just kept on jabbering. Nana interrupted with more instruction, "Once the oil is hot, ya drop the dough inta the hot oil and watch it sizzle 'round the edge as it cooks."

The kid had just enrolled in Nana's donut home school class. She continued, "The hot oil will turn the donut brown, first on one side then ya flip 'em over an' cook 'em on the other side." She then explained how to get a glaze on the donuts, "The way you do this is drizzle Karo corn sugar syrup on top and down the sides, especially as they's real hot." Nana and the kid finished making donuts, and then ate them all. Well, Grandpa did help a little in eating them.

After a breakfast of donuts and eggs, Dakota, still thinking about the dress-up game, went outside to be alone. He walked around but didn't go far, just to the alley and around the pepper trees. With not much to do, he was bored so he went in the storage room/garage to see what was happening in there. Leaning against the wall was a big machete knife, almost nearly as tall as he was. As Dakota tried to swing this massive knife, he quickly learned it took both hands to manage it. Swinging it around in the air wasn't much fun. Dakota thought, "What can I cut?" The first thing Dakota saw as he exited the storage room with the twenty-inch blade was a banana tree. It was planted in an old worn out tire serving as a flower pot. It wasn't too big a tree and Dakota wanted to see how sharp the knife was. The kid set his sights on the little tree.

Dakota took a quick look around to see if anyone was watching. The coast was clear. With both hands, that little kid took a swing, whacking the blade at the trunk of the banana tree. The blade went deep in the small green trunk. Not satisfied, he took another whack and with the third whack the tree toppled over and Dakota was delighted with his accomplishment. The kid proudly put away the machete knowing this would be his little secret from Nana because secrets were okay, especially if you were doing something wrong.

But in this case Dakota didn't understand the concept of evidence. The tree stump and the tree lying on the ground would hardly remain a secret.

Dakota went back to the safe cover of the pepper trees, and realized the fun of cutting the banana tree down wasn't all that much fun after all. Now he was kind of sad he had done it.

Like so many weekends at Nana's, the kid just hung around, listening to sounds of cars and airplanes, sometimes talking to Coach just to pass the time.

THREE
Changing Dakota

The banana tree came down

The banana tree lay lifeless on the ground next to the place where it once stood. Dakota was just waiting around to see what his punishment would be that Saturday morning.

About that time a big cloud of exhaust smoke billowed up from the alley. An old Chevrolet sedan emerged from the dust and smoke, bouncing its way over the bumps toward Nana's. It was the Stockman family—Nana's brother, Raymond. This guy was tougher than steel. Raymond came around Nana's house often. This visit included Raymond's wife, Inez, and their boys Don Lee and John Eddie. This family could have been real nice, but they all looked downright scary, dangerous even, like an old fashioned wanted poster.

Inez, the mom, was as skinny as a stick. The two boys were dressed in bib overalls, no shirt, and brown, tore-up high-top boots. Both of the boys looked like they would kill you if you even so much as looked at them funny. Raymond, the dad, was also in bib overalls but he dressed it up a notch with a white T-shirt under the overalls. Raymond was big, tall and strong. He looked like some folklore lumberjack. Dakota didn't like to get close to this bunch of hooligans who looked and acted more like a gang of moonshiners than a family. They scared the piss out of the young Dakota.

All of them were walking up the path toward the house. Dakota, standing a safe distance from them, heard Nana yell out the back door, "Dakota, what the hell happened to my banana tree?" The kid turned red and Raymond and everyone broke out in laughter such as the kid had never seen.

While everyone was laughing at the downed tree, Nana said, "Laugh now because Grandpa Mike won't be laughing when he gets home." Looking directly at Dakota, she asked, "How the hell did ya cut the tree down?" Raymond and the boys couldn't stop laughing; it was so funny. The kid explained, "There's a big knife in the storage room and I used the big knife." Nana said, "That's Uncle Tiny's machete he brought back from the war. Stay away from the storage room and don't go in there again."

Nana was talking about her son, brother to Dakota's mother, Ellie. Everyone called him "Tiny" because he was so short. He wore a size four-and-a-half shoe and was just a bit taller than a "little person." So much for all things from Texas being big. Nana was trying to look angry but as she looked again at the tree on the ground she broke out into laughter, too, because it was so funny.

Nana told Dakota: "Take a ride with Inez. She's goin' to the grocery store. We need some food for supper."

Nana called the meal at lunchtime "supper" and the meal at dinner time, "dinner." Supper, to most people Dakota knew, was at dinner time. Anyway, that was Nana Texas talk, the kid thought.

After Inez talked to Nana about the groceries they needed, she came outside. She and Dakota got in the old rattletrap Bonnie and Clyde car and off they went. Dakota wasn't sure if this was his punishment for cutting down the little tree or not. Dakota quickly noticed some of the floorboards were missing and he could see a big hole in the passenger-side wood floor right below his seat. Dakota looked down and watched the asphalt under his feet as the road passed by. The four-year-old kid was choking on the smoke from the car's exhaust fumes.

Inez was like Nana; she just went on sipping that whiskey from the bottle she had tucked under her leg on the front seat. Inez looked like she hadn't had any food in months. But Inez always looked like death warmed over. Anyway, this little kid was coughing so bad he couldn't talk. Dakota made a mental note that if there was a next time, he would refuse to ride with Inez. That Stockman bunch was just not normal, but neither was Nana. This was the wild bunch, for sure.

Raymond and his family stayed for supper (lunch). Dakota was bored out of his mind—no more banana trees to cut down. So he just sat under the pepper tree alone, a safe distance from everyone. Dakota liked baking apple pie with Nana but there would be no pie baking on this day. Grandpa Mike, when told of the fallen banana tree, kindly said, "That little old tree needed cutting down anyway" but he did tell Dakota never to pick up that knife again because it was dangerous and that was the end of Dakota touching the knife.

The day passed. The Stockman family drove off in the same cloud of dust they rode in on. Dinner was finished and Grandpa Mike was preparing for a long distance towing job that would take hours. He was out the door as soon as dinner was over.

As evening came on Dakota grew even more restless thinking Nana would play the dress-up game again. Dakota had hoped Grandpa would stay home this Saturday night but he wouldn't be there. Little Dakota was in the front room, sitting in a chair at a table coloring with crayons in a Hopalong Cassidy coloring book trying to stay in the lines when Nana called out, "I got something for ya. Come to the back porch and get up on top of this round cushion." Dakota did as Nana asked. He didn't know what was about to happen but Nana looked real happy.

In retrospect, many years later, Dakota would see the events of this day as a powerful and critical point in his impressionable psyche. The four-year-old boy was placed atop a round foot-cushion, a pedestal of sorts. Nana, knowingly or unknowingly, was telegraphing a powerful message to Dakota: "You're okay as a boy, but it would be better if you were a girl." That pedestal, in concert with the dress-up game, was where Nana started the process of transforming the boy Dakota into a girl.

As harmless as it seemed to Nana, the game she was playing planted the seed of doubt in Dakota about his gender at a time so crucial and pivotal to a young boy's development. It was no longer just a game, but brain washing. Slowly, reinforced over time, doubts would grow in Dakota about whether he is a boy or a girl. Nana manipulated this boy's core identity and psyche at a time when it wasn't yet fully developed.

Nana had made clothing for years. This time she pulled open a drawer in her sewing cabinet and removed a bundle of soft material with a flower pattern. She asked Dakota, "Do you like this material? Feel it." The young kid smiled, "Wow, it feels real soft, Nana." Then Nana got a big smile on her face as she told the boy, "It's time ya got your own dress, one that fits ya perfectly and I'm gonna make it for ya. It'll be our little secret. Don't even tell your grandpa." Dakota agreed, "Okay." By telling the boy, "This is our secret game of dress up" Nana introduced him to a gender seductive game that would now include a specially made dress for Dakota. This wasn't the first time Nana played dress-up with Dakota, but this was the first time Nana intensified the level of her desire to see him as a girl by making him his own dress.

The kid thought it was great to get so much special attention. He was allowed to stand on the cushion while Nana measured his height, waist and dress length. At the first fitting, Dakota started getting this tingling feeling all over. Dakota sensed he was changing. Nana told her grandson, "The next time ya come for the weekend, I'll have the dress all finished and ready for ya. Ya'll look like a beautiful little girl."

Dakota was excited when he went to bed and called on his imaginary friend, Coach. Dakota needed answers. "Coach, what do you think of the dress Nana's making for me?" Coach was thoughtful in his reply: "I don't think Nana making you a dress so you look like a girl is a good thing." Dakota said, "Really? Maybe she was dressing me because I told her how much I liked the way it made me feel. The material is soft. It feels better than boy's clothes."

Coach wasn't buying it: "You're a little boy. Your grandma must have wanted a girl." Dakota kept trying to convince Coach, "I'm small, not big at all like most boys. I think I should have been born a girl; it feels so good to me." Coach, "Your Nana is trying to change you. Maybe she just doesn't like men or boys." Back and forth, Dakota and Coach went on.

Over the next several months, Dakota had more stay-overs and games of dress-up, but Nana hadn't finished the dress yet. In October Dakota turned five. Surely Nana has finished the dress, he thought. Had the old gal changed her mind? Did she forget? What was taking so long? Finally, weeks later, Dakota was there when Grandpa Mike was gone on a towing job. Nana motioned to her grandson saying, "Dakota, come 'ere. I want ta show ya somethin'." The young boy followed Nana to the old musty closet that stunk like a locker room. Nana said with a smile, "Come on now; take off your clothes. I have something for ya."

Nana unfolded the most beautiful little girl dress the boy had ever seen. He couldn't take his eyes off of it. Nana asked Dakota, "Would ya like to try it on?" The boy couldn't say no. Hearing Dakota say yes, Nana helped him slip into that dress. A boy in a handmade girl's dress. By this time the dress was becoming like sweet candy. Dakota liked the way it made him feel. Over the next several months at Nana's house, opportunities for the dress-up game popped up whenever Grandpa Mike was away and Nana was alone with her grandson. That's when Nana would slip that handmade little dress over Dakota's small slender body.

No doubt Nana had no thoughts beyond the moment. She didn't thoughtfully consider the possibility of the kid's future or any consequences that could arise in the months and years to come from dressing up as a girl. It was so simple. It seemed so harmless. Dakota was enjoying all the attention Nana gave him over his female clothing. Whenever Grandpa Mike wasn't there, Nana encouraged and guided Dakota every step of the way to wear the dress. Dakota was a small-framed, sensitive boy. It wasn't likely he would tell Nana to stop the dress-up game after all this time. He had learned to enjoy being the center of her attention.

Dakota was starting to have doubts about whether he was a boy. Could one dress change one boy?

Nana's game of dress-up was repeated time and time again, giving the young boy the idea he was better as a girl than a boy. Dakota's identity at ages four and five was still under development. It was still at a point where it could be molded and altered by someone like Nana. This boy was under the care and custody of his grandma. His mom, papa and even Dakota himself trusted his life to Nana. After all, he was just a little kid.

The dress-up game was a well-kept secret so far, but that was about to change. Nana should have known such secrets are hard to keep, especially if one of the keepers of the secret was a child. Dakota had changed in the year that Nana played dress-up with him. On his visits to Nana's he was withdrawn and silent. He'd just sit in silence under the big pepper tree and think about the secret he couldn't talk about with anyone except Coach. Dakota wasn't playing as much with the other kids. He spent more time thinking about how he looked in that new dress and more time alone trying to push the image out of his head.

Dakota started his own game, one he called the listening game. The purpose of the game was to sit quietly and drown out the obsessive thoughts by listening to different sounds and try to identify each sound. This game was the only way to push the thoughts of the girl's dress out of his head. Dakota would just sit quietly and listen to the sounds, telling his friend, Coach, what each sound was: "That was a big truck." "That was an old Chevy like Uncle Raymond's." "That's a military plane way up in the sky."

Dakota listened to sounds as a way to escape constantly thinking about playing dress-up at Nana's house. Dakota couldn't stop thinking about playing dress-up. It became more and more difficult for this young boy child to push away his desires to slip into that little dress Nana made for him. Even when he wasn't at Nana's, he wanted to slip into the dress.

Dakota listened to lots of sounds to push away thoughts of how smooth and soft that little dress felt on his skin. Some nights, when this boy was in his own bed at home, he just lay there listening to sounds, some from the massive Los Angeles train hub and switching yard three miles away. In the silence of night, sounds of the trains easily traveled three miles: horns blowing, steel wheels rolling over train tracks, the crushing sound made when the box cars slammed steel on steel to connect and lock, one to another, that sound was the loudest. The sounds of the trains were as much a friend to this young boy as Coach during the long nights because they replaced the thoughts of the dress. Dakota lay there listening and thinking. He would say to Coach, "I wish I didn't have the feelings or even think about the dress." The young kid was now at a low point as he shared his feelings with Coach, "I wish the game and the dress had never happened to me."

Dakota's older brother, Danny, always fell asleep fast. He blissfully snored away the night only a few feet from Dakota in the bedroom they shared. Two very different childhoods were developing in the home. The brothers were in the same family, but their experiences were very different. Dakota had way too much to think about. He couldn't sleep. He wished he could sleep like his big brother.

Sounds remained the antidote to Dakota's thought life. A plane, a train, emergency sirens from police or fire blasting away provided a good distraction for troubling thoughts. Dakota wanted Coach to answer his deep questions. He asked him, "Coach, why do I feel this way? How can I make the girl feelings go away when I like them? Coach was sometimes not much help when he said things like, "Dakota, this is too confusing. You're a boy. Why did Nana make you a dress when you're a boy? She must be crazy." Coach had a few questions for Dakota himself: "Dakota, do you think Nana's dress-up game is good for you just because it is fun?" Dakota squirmed a little as he replied, "It makes me feel good and she smiles. That's all I know." Then the kid asked Coach the big question, "Should I tell my papa and mom about the dress and the dress-up game?" Coach was certain in his advice, "The only way to know if playing dress-up is good for you is to tell Mom and Papa. You just got to tell them, Dakota. You got to do it."

When Nana played the dress-up game, she always told Dakota, "Ya look wonderful as a girl." Five-year-old Dakota was confused because Nana didn't say, "I love ya as a boy. That's really what you are." She never did that. She never said anything positive about him being a boy. Nana always talked about, "Ya look so cute as a girl." It didn't matter what Dakota initially thought about the game of dress up. Under Nana's influence the non-combative, sensitive youngster became a little ball of Silly

Putty especially after she made that dress for him. Dakota was easy to shape into the girl she envisioned.

The boy's young mind was impressionable to the point he was starting to feel he had been born wrong. Maybe he really was a girl. With that secret came increased pressure to hide behind his feelings. Talking silently to his imaginary friend Coach and losing himself in distant sounds were the only safe places for the boy's thoughts to go. Otherwise the doubts about whether he was a girl or a boy were constant. Kid Dakota now knew the only way he felt good about himself was to slip into that special dress. Then Nana would love him and he would love himself. This grandchild found over time he just didn't feel loved as a boy but he did as a girl.

The sounds did take up all the space in his head. It was a temporary reprieve, but better than nothing. It was better, he thought, to listen to car tires rolling across the pavement, car exhaust noise, a horn blowing or people talking in the distance than it was to be obsessed by the little dress Nana made for him. Hearing the sounds of kids playing and laughing made him wish it was his laughter. Kid Dakota was starting to feel like he was different than all the other kids. He had this secret about a dress he couldn't talk about it.

The sounds of the Helms Bakery truck coming down the street, its whistle filling the air, signaled the presence of baked goods nearby, like yummy cookies, bread and cinnamon rolls. The best sound, however, to the kids on Dakota's street was the music of the Good Humor ice cream truck on hot summer afternoons. The jingle from the Good Humor truck was so loud the children could hear it coming from blocks away. That jingle from the Good Humor truck played over and over and over, and soon many of the kids were happily holding their ice cream bars. They no longer cared that the truck drove away and the sound of the jingle faded in the distance. The mint and chocolate chip bar covered in milk chocolate was Dakota's favorite.

One sound manufactured by Dakota was actually a kids' invention: making his bicycle, a staple in every kid's life, sound like a motor. The main requirements were three or four wooden clothespins (no clothes dryers back then) and three or four Bicycle brand playing cards. To make the sound, Dakota bent the edge of each playing card over the fender brace so it was in a position to hit the spokes on the bicycle wheel and secured it with a clothespin. The playing cards would strike the spokes on the wheel as it turned to make a motor-like sound.

This young boy was trying to act as if he were normal, but that wasn't easy when his Nana was telling him that he looked better as a girl. Coach's voice in his head was telling him he needed to talk to his mom and papa about the secret. That wasn't so easy. Dakota didn't know how he would tell them. He was scared to tell them because Nana told him not to tell anyone, not his parents, not even Grandpa Mike.

This remarkable boy, in spite of his Nana's actions, appeared to be the happiest kid on the block. He made people laugh with his great sense of humor. He was engaging to talk with but completely unaware or mature enough to know how to deal with Nana or his growing girl feelings. Over a year had passed since that first night of dress-up, a long time for a young boy to keep the secret of a game he was starting to enjoy.

Dakota had become so involved and excited about playing dress-up he wanted to bring the dress home and start wearing the dress all the time. So on one return trip, waving goodbye to Nana, he climbed into the family car with the dress secretly tucked into the paper bag that served as his overnight suitcase. He had no grasp of the outcome from bringing the secret home with him. That bag grasped firmly in his hand held the flowered print dress Nana had made for him. The secret would be revealed. This confused but lovable little boy knew he needed to tell his mom and papa. He just wasn't sure how to do that.

Dakota didn't tell Nana the dress was going home with him this day. He knew she'd be mad if she knew. Better not to tell her. Soon Mom and Papa would know. At this point this youngster was carrying the weight of his secret world on his shoulders. Nothing could calm him, not the sounds game, nor even talking with Coach.

Once Papa and Dakota got home, the kid walked swiftly toward his bedroom with the hidden dress in the bag wondering how he would tell Mom and Papa about the dress. Days passed; a week passed. Dakota couldn't get the words in his mouth and spit out what he needed to tell his mom and dad.

This was a heavy weight to carry and it needed to be offloaded.

FOUR

The Dress in the Drawer

Uncle Kyle with a neighborhood boy

Dakota kept thinking about that dress tucked away in his dresser drawer, knowing he would be going back to Nana's soon. What if Nana discovered he took the dress home? He just couldn't find the words he needed to tell his mom and dad.

After dinner the three of them, Mom, Papa and Dakota, were sitting at the family table. No one was saying much of anything. Brother Danny was outside in the backyard. Dakota felt tension in the silence, like a bubble about to burst. Mom, Papa and

Dakota just sat there at the table when suddenly the silence was broken. But it wasn't Dakota that broke that icy silence; it was Mom. "Tell me, young man, why do you have a dress hidden in the bottom drawer of your dresser?"

Dakota was caught off guard. Mom Ellie had discovered the secret dress and she sounded angry. A sinking feeling in the pit of his stomach left him speechless, not knowing what to say. Then Papa, with even a stronger more forceful voice, said: "Answer your mother. Where did you get that damn dress and whose dress is it?" The kid was stunned and shaken, even though he knew this day would come. He gasped for a breath. Hesitating, trying to delay answering, he took a deep breath, then blurted, "It's my dress. Nana made it for me a long time ago. I wear it when I'm at her house and now I want to wear it at home."

Papa jumped up from the table like he had been shot from a cannon. In an angry, stunned voice, he said "Oh, my God." Over and over: "O, my God. O my God." Papa stomped straight to the front screen door, furious. He threw open the door and flew out. A loud bang followed as the door slammed shut behind him. It sounded like he put all his strength and force into the action.

Mom's head dropped as she started crying. Slowly she pushed back from the dinner table and walked into her bedroom, quietly closing the door behind her. The contrast in how they responded wasn't lost that night even on this young boy.

Now this kid was real scared because they didn't even know about the secret dress-up game yet. The young boy was caught between pleasing a grandma who enjoyed dressing her grandson in a dress, and the wrath of his mom and papa; not a good place to be. That was really frightening. Dakota fled to his room. Lying on his bed flat on his face, crying, he started talking to his imaginary friend, Coach. "This is all my fault. I made Papa mad and Mom cry. Nana will hate me because she told me not to tell." Coach responded, "It's a mess, but you should have told them about Nana's dress-up game the very first time you played it with her."

Now the little boy was heartbroken; the dress had been the spark that set off huge fireworks. Crying and feeling sick to his stomach he asked Coach, "Why did Nana dress me like a girl? I'm in big trouble now. Is it my fault?"

After a bit, Dakota could hear Papa come back in the house. It sounded like he was walking toward the bedrooms. He stopped first to talk to Mom, who was still crying in their bedroom. The first words Dakota overheard Papa say to Mom scared the young boy. Papa was telling Mom, "That boy will never stay over at your mom's again. Don't even ask me to think about it." Dakota was listening to the sounds of trouble.

Mom started walking toward the kitchen, her shoes making noise on the hardwood floors. Papa's footsteps were close behind hers. Mom told Papa, "I can't talk to you now. You're too upset. Just go away. Leave me alone." Listening, Dakota could hear Papa was still angry. Papa told her, "You will listen to me and yes, I'm angry. Your mother isn't welcome here in our house ever again." Mom tearfully replied, "Just go away please; just go away." Papa then told Mom, "Your mother is a crazy woman! Who in their right mind would make a dress for their grandson? Tell me—who would do that?" Papa went out the back door to the back yard this time, slamming the door. Papa always slammed doors when he was angry and he was very upset and angry now.

Mom was now crying uncontrollably. She went back to her bedroom. This little kid listened to all the sounds of fighting, crying, slamming of doors, and yelling. It hurt deeply to listen to these sounds. He covered his ears with a bed pillow in an effort to muffle the reverberation of all this bad stuff.

After a few minutes Dakota removed the pillow from his ears and looked up. Standing there was Papa, like a chiseled statue hovering over him. Papa could see there in bed was just a little kid, his youngest son, no girl there. Papa needed to take charge of this. In a drill sergeant voice, Papa said, "Where is the dress? Tell me. Where is the dress?" Dakota was scared and started crying again and choked out his reply, "I-i-n the drawer." Papa walked over to the dresser. He opened one drawer—no dress there. He tried the next drawer and there it was. Papa pulled the dress out. The kid could see through his tears how angry Papa was and how tight a grip Papa had on that dress. It could have crushed cold steel.

Out of the bedroom Papa strode, the dress in his grasp, never to be seen again. No more Nana stay-overs for his boy. No more little dress for Papa's youngest son. Dakota could hear Papa say to Mom, "His nana won't make a sissy out of my boy. She cannot be with him unless I'm there." With those parting words, Papa was out the front door again, got in his car and drove off.

Dakota was sad because he liked having Nana's special attention. Yet at the same time, it cut Dakota deeply that Nana never liked him as a boy. He couldn't tell her because he didn't want to hurt her.

The kid was shaken to his core, not knowing what to do. He was scared. He knew Nana had done something very wrong. That much he did know. He also knew Nana would be very mad at him for telling about the dress, so it was good he wouldn't see Nana alone again. Dakota stayed under the covers in bed that evening, still fully dressed, trying to muffle the sounds of renewed arguing between Mom and Papa.

As bedtime approached, Dakota put on his pajamas and crawled back in bed where it felt safe. Big brother Danny came into the bedroom and whispered, "You're in deep trouble, little buddy." Danny didn't know about the dress; he just knew his little brother was in trouble. Danny didn't know Nana had made the dress or dressed his brother in girl's clothes. Danny only knew from all the yelling that his little brother was in trouble. Danny was still in the bedroom when Mom and Papa walked in just moments later. Papa dismissed Danny, "Go into the living room and wait until I call you, after we're done talking to Dakota." Danny left the bedroom.

Papa sat on the edge of Dakota's bed. Mom sat at the end of the bed. Dad spoke first. "Your nana was wrong to make you that dress. It will never happen again; I promise you, son." Mom tried to comfort him, "We are so sorry this has happened to you. Nana never should have done what she did. It wasn't your fault. You're a boy and boys don't wear dresses." Dakota remained quiet as Papa spoke again, "There'll be no more talk about the dress in this house."

Papa called for Danny to come back in the bedroom to join them. As a family, the four of them were in the bedroom for nightly prayer time. For the first time ever, Papa said the nightly prayer: "Now I lay me down to sleep. I pray the Lord my soul to take. If I should die before I wake, I pray the Lord my soul to take. Amen." Then Papa wanted everyone in the family to know, "There will be no more discussion or talk about Dakota being in trouble because he isn't in trouble."

The troubled little boy crawled under covers that night crying and trembling. Only a week ago, Dakota had felt the euphoric excitement of playing dress-up at Nana's and hiding the dress in his bag to bring it home. Now he felt that things would never be the same again and that hurt. It was a catastrophe. He had no one to talk to about it; Dad had made it clear the topic was off-limits.

After the horrible evening, the next morning came as usual. The boys went off to school, happy to be out of the house. Going to school today was a relief. Dakota wasn't really sure if his brother Danny had heard about the dress. If he did, would he keep his big mouth shut? Papa did remind Danny not to tell the other kids that Dakota got in big trouble. Back at school, Dakota found some fun things to do with his friends. He started to feel better, laughing and enjoying his friends and putting the awful memory behind him.

From now on, when Mom and Papa went away, Dakota stayed and played at the home of Papa's parents, Grandpa Clint and Grandma Florence ("Flossie") Martin. No longer would Dakota have to watch longingly as his older brother, Danny, ran around the corner to their house for the weekend. As far as Dakota was concerned, this turn of events was a good thing. He had no desire to see Nana or talk to her. It was more fun to build balsa wood models with Grandpa Clint and Danny. These grandparents had a real nice home; no junkyard behind their house. Most importantly, the Martins never said anything about the dress-up game or the dress, so maybe they didn't know about it.

A few weeks later, the extended family gathered for a family get-together at Grandpa Clint's. Everyone on the Martin side of the family turned out, including Dakota's teenage uncle named Kyle who was a troublemaker. Kyle had been adopted by the Martins because Flossie's older sister got pregnant by an American Indian boy. Unwed motherhood was a scandal that needed to be covered up.

Somehow that afternoon Uncle Kyle caught wind of Dakota getting dressed up like a girl. This was the last person he needed to know about that. Uncle Kyle got Dakota alone just so he could make fun of the kid. Kyle started by using a silly squeaky voice to scare Dakota, "I know you are a sissy—you had a dress." Dakota begged his uncle, "Stop calling me a sissy; please don't do that." Uncle Kyle was so delighted with himself; he just laughed and quickly grabbed Dakota's trousers with both hands. With one swift jerk he pulled Dakota's pants down around his little ankles. Then Kyle laughed all the more.

As fast as lightning Dakota pulled his pants up and ran into the house for safety. Once inside he sat in his quiet mode, listening to the sounds of people talking and laughing, the clamor of pots and pans being used to prepare the big dinner. Dakota had escaped from his uncle's unwanted abuse into his solitary world of sounds again. He spent the remainder of the day avoiding his uncle.

Dakota had always been a skinny kid but after the reveal of the dress, the ensuing blow-up between Mom and Papa, and Uncle Kyle's bullying, this kid became an eating machine. Kid Dakota ate seven tuna fish sandwiches at lunch and huge amounts at dinner; he couldn't get enough food. The kids at school gave Dakota the nickname of "Butterball" because of how fat he was getting. It was just the way it was.

Over the next several months Uncle Kyle ramped up the number of times he would pull down Dakota's pants and laugh. Kyle would watch for opportunities to pull Dakota's pants down when kids were around, just to humiliate him. He taunted and laughed at Dakota, "You're a sissy boy with a dress. Ha. Ha." Grabbing and downing Dakota's pants wasn't enough for this teenage troublemaker. He went further, touching and fondling Dakota's private parts, laughing at how small he was down there. Kyle's teasing and groping went on time and time again. The repeated abuses by his uncle were deeply hurtful and difficult to ignore. Dakota didn't fight back. He felt like everyone was hurting him: Nana, Papa and Mom, Uncle Kyle, and the kids at school who called him "Butterball."

One afternoon Uncle Kyle came over in his V8 Ford. He parked his car on the narrow street in front of Dakota's house, walked up the stairs and knocked on the door. Mom Ellie opened the door and Kyle started his sales pitch: "Can Dakota come for a little ride up in the hills behind the house? We'll only be an hour or so. Just a fun joyride." Mom didn't see any harm in it. "Sure, he can go."

Mom yelled into the house, "Dakota, Kyle is here. He wants to take you for a ride on the roads behind the house."

Dakota came out of his room into the hall and yelled back, "I don't want to go."

Mom urged him, "Go; get out of the house. You've been inside too long."

Dakota resisted, saying, "I really don't want to go."

Mom told him again, "You can't sit around all day. Now get out of here and go with Kyle. It'll be fun."

Walking to the door where Kyle stood, without a word, Dakota squeezed his chubby self between Mom and Kyle and headed down the walkway to the car. He opened the door on Uncle Kyle's Ford and plopped himself in the front passenger seat as Kyle jumped behind the wheel next to the kid.

The two drove into the hills behind the house on roads carved into the landscape—narrow, well-hidden dirt roads that opened up at times into clearings. At one of these openings, Uncle Kyle, who was a big show off, wanted to demonstrate his skill at doing "brodies" in the dirt. Dakota's crazy uncle was shouting, "I'm gonna do a brodie!" Then he accelerated and jerked the steering wheel hard to the right. The car spun in a circle, doing a "brodie." Dakota wasn't keen on this, and complained, "You're going too fast. Slow down, please." His wacko uncle laughed, "This is so much fun. Just hang on!" as he quickly turned the steering wheel all the way left, causing the car to spin and slinging a dirt rooster tail into the air. Dirt flew everywhere. The dust piled up until Dakota couldn't see or take a breath. Dakota wasn't a cheerleader for this, and said disbelievingly, "That's what you call fun?"

At that, Uncle Kyle's mood turned nasty. "You're no fun at all, Dakota. No fun at all." He drove a short distance down a hidden dirt road and stopped the car. He sneered at Dakota, "Take off your clothes." This was too much for Dakota. It made him angry and he stood up for himself. "No, I won't take off my clothes. Why are you doing this? Why?" Kyle again said, "Take off your clothes." Tauntingly, he said to his nephew, "I have a dress for you, sissy boy." Then the teen uncle forced Dakota to take off his shoes, his shirt and his pants, leaving him only in his underwear and socks. Reaching out, Kyle pressed his hand on the boy's underwear over his penis. Dakota was scared. High in the hills, at the mercy of his crazy uncle, away from any source of help, and forcibly undressed, Dakota realized the danger of his situation. In desperation, he opened the door of that old V8 Ford and took off running down the winding dusty dirt road toward his house, dressed only in his underwear and socks.

When Dakota finally reached the edge of his neighborhood, he ducked behind a big bush beside the road and hid, his heart pounding. Dakota knew Kyle would be looking for him soon. He listened for the sound of the old Ford. He heard the car coming slowly in his direction. Uncle Kyle called out the driver-side window in a sing-song voice, like he was looking for a lost cat, "Dakota, Dakota, where are you?" Just then the old Ford was visible and Dakota yelled back, "I'm over here. Now give me my clothes back." The uncle wanted no part of anyone discovering what he had done. Out the car window went the clothes. They landed near the bush where Dakota was hiding. Once he had tossed the clothes out of the car, Kyle sped away. Another chapter in the book of Dakota's life lessons was written that day. Dakota couldn't trust people; they always hurt him. Something must be wrong with him to cause all these bad things to happen to him.

Dakota grabbed his clothes off the ground and quickly got dressed behind the bush. As fast as his legs would carry him, he ran for home. He had learned his lesson about keeping secrets; this time, he would tell Mom right away. Dakota flew in the back door and entered the kitchen where Mom was. Quick as Dakota could get his breath to speak he said, "Mom, Mom, Uncle Kyle made me take off my clothes and he grabbed me here," pointing to his pee pee. Mom Ellie rolled her eyes like he was telling a fairy tale. "You're making that up. Your uncle would never do that.

You're just saying that because you didn't want to go. Now go to your room and stay there." Dakota walked away, his shoulders drooped in defeat. Mom wasn't quite finished and called after him, "You got to stop lying, Dakota." This kid was getting it from all sides.

In his room, sitting on the edge of his bed, Dakota felt alone and at a loss as to how to handle all that had come at him recently: put in a dress and warmly accepted by Nana, followed by the nuclear explosion when his parents learned about it; having his pants pulled down, being humiliated and touched "down there" by his uncle; telling the truth and being called a liar by Mom. It was all too much. He thought to himself, "How am I supposed to know what is right when everything turns out so darn wrong? If I keep the secret too long, I get into trouble. But if I let Mom know right away, she doesn't believe me and calls me a liar." Dakota was starting to wonder if he could do anything right.

When Papa got home, Mom told him Dakota's story. Papa was stern with Dakota and said, "I'm going to talk to Kyle and you better not be lying about this one because I'm sick and tired of all that's going on with you." As if all that was going on was the boy's fault.

Papa walked the short distance to his parents' house around the corner so he could talk to Kyle. When Papa came home he went straight to Dakota's room. "You made it all up. He just took you for a joyride in the hills and that was all." What a bad day. Dakota had been abused, bullied and hurt and the kid felt like no one cared. The kid was crying and saying over and over again to Papa, "I told the truth. Why is he lying? Why is he lying?" Papa just pointed his finger at Dakota and shouted, "Just stay in your room until I can figure out what punishment will be best for you."

At least big brother Danny wasn't at home; Dakota took some comfort in that.

Papa thought Dakota needed to be disciplined. The adults around Dakota thought Dakota was always lying. Dakota didn't have anyone he could trust or talk to, not even Coach because the advice from Coach to "tell your parents about the dress" turned out so horrible. He no longer wanted advice from Coach. So Dakota, older now, grew out of talking to Coach, his imaginary friend. But the truth was Dakota had no place to turn for help; he was alone.

Papa's discipline for lying was the trusted old hardwood floor plank across his son's bare butt cheeks. Papa believed his adopted brother Kyle told the truth and that led to only one conclusion: Dakota was a liar. So the kid took the harsh discipline his uncle deserved. Papa was a man's man and discipline for children was a normal practice. Discipline by a hardwood floor plank was common in that day also. The plank always came calling. Dakota knew the drill: pants down, exposing a bare skin butt. Bend over slightly and place hands on knees. Then brace for the awful impact. The hardwood floor plank moved through the air swiftly with a whack, then another. This level of discipline wasn't new to the kid; it was routine. Mom Ellie was no lightweight either. She had leveled her own brand of harsh discipline many times. So it is easy to understand Dakota wasn't surprised that his tender little butt would come in contact with the oak hardwood floor plank. So what if there were new welts? Dakota was just disappointed it wasn't his uncle who was getting whacked.

Neither Mom nor Papa would sit down and listen to their young boy. No, they dismissed his words as lies and it hurt him deeply. Dakota had been telling the truth all along but his parents wouldn't even consider that Kyle had been taunting and teasing their boy. Was it possible the bond of trust between Dakota and his parents had been broken over the secret at Nana's? Perhaps the parents just don't trust their boy. Dakota needed unimaginable internal strength just to keep that little smile and his great sense of humor.

Some great times were interspersed in among the bad in young Dakota's life. One of those was on a family vacation in the summer when Dakota was seven. Papa was a great outdoorsman and he liked to take Dakota and Danny fishing, camping and hiking. Papa and Mom showed the boys some outstanding vacations to the national parks, driving there in the old '41 Ford.

On a hike in Yosemite, Dakota was so taken by the amazing beauty of nature around him he failed to see a rock at his feet. He tripped and fell hard, suffering a compound fracture to his right wrist. But Papa wasn't upset with Dakota. Papa quickly picked his boy up and ran to the car with him in his arms. He drove his boy to the park medical station where they set Dakota's wrist and wrapped it in a heavy white cast. This mishap caused the family's vacation to end early. But Dakota counted it as a great experience. He may have broken his wrist, but the memory of resting in Papa's arms set Dakota to thinking, "Mom and Papa, they do love me." This was the first time in a long time Dakota felt loved.

Nana, Uncle Kyle, Papa and Mom all were helping, in good ways or bad, to shape Dakota's young life. This little kid was off to a very rough start. Dakota started to feel like he was just a toy for adults to play with—not a good feeling. But this tough kid was determined, no matter what, to forge his way through this tough time.

Images from his experiences formed indelible impressions that Dakota couldn't easily dismiss, especially the image of him standing on a cushion as Nana began to fashion for him a little flowered print dress. As much as this young boy attempted to dismiss the images and feelings, he couldn't make them go away. The dress itself was gone, never returned to his dresser drawer, but the seed of desire that it planted in Dakota grew. More and more, he imagined slipping into that little dress. This young child now wanted his own dress so he could play dress up any time he wanted. No Nana this time; not even Coach. Dakota wanted this secret for himself.

Dakota also had a budding cowboy inside him. He loved cowboy boots, western clothing and the sounds of guitar music. This love for anything western was due in part to the popular western singer on the radio, Gene Autry. Dakota's mom and her friend, Margaret, enjoyed making western wear as a hobby. Dakota's little house had tables filled with material, shirt patterns and sewing machines, all the necessary tools to make fancy western shirts. Margaret was an artist when it came to painting or embroidering elaborate big red flowers on the western wear.

Margaret's young daughter, Peggy, was the same age as Dakota, and she, too, loved the sound of western music. One of the most popular weekly television shows in the late 1940s was The Spade Cooley Show which featured popular western swing music. The real star of the show as far as Dakota and Peggy were concerned was the guy most visible on stage, Speedy West. He played the electric steel guitar behind every song. Peggy told her dad Sax (who was a real cowboy) and Dakota told his papa that they wanted to learn how to play the electric steel guitar like Speedy West on television.

Papa liked the idea and found out from his brother-in-law that Speedy West taught electric steel guitar in his studio on the second floor over the paint and hardware store in Pasadena, nice and close to home. Both Papa and Sax made arrangements to talk with Speedy West about music lessons for the two kids. When the dads learned the lessons cost two dollars for a one hour session, they agreed this was a good opportunity for both kids. Using rental guitars, both kids took to learning the electric steel guitar like it was in their DNA. Peggy and Dakota were very competitive, one always trying to outdo the other. The result was they both were learning very fast. In just a few short months Dakota had mastered playing his favorite music arrangement "Electric Steel Guitar Rag" and Speedy West invited him to play the song on his radio show. Dakota was so excited he asked his mom to make him a fancy western shirt to wear for the show.

Dakota's mom and Peggy's mom, Margaret, worked together to make two fancy western shirts, one for Dakota and one for Peggy. Dakota's shirt was gray and silver with bright green piping to highlight the western design. Dakota loved the shirt. It was perfect for playing western music. He couldn't wait to wear it for the show.

The radio appearance was still weeks away, so Dakota wore his new shirt when the family went out to dinner that Friday night. Sitting at the table in the restaurant, Papa turned toward Mom, and clearly showing his dislike for the shirt Dakota was wearing, asked her, "Why did you make that shirt for him? It looks like a sissy shirt." With that, Papa sucked down his second martini.

Sure, Papa wanted his boy to look like a boy but the words cut deep and even hurt Mom. No doubt because she was the one who helped Peggy's mom, Margaret, to make it.

What should have been a special moment was, instead, a bruising blow to the kid's identity. The hurt went so deep to Dakota's core that he never put the shirt on again. Broken by Papa's searing words, Dakota didn't go on Speedy West's radio show or ever play the electric steel guitar again. He was good, but he was done. Nana's actions and Papa's words had become too much. The thoughtlessly harsh words from his beloved Papa squeezed the excitement and joy from the kid's heart. Kid Dakota, the western guitar playing young cowboy, loved music and wanted to keep playing, but didn't want to be called a sissy ever again. It hurt too much. Everyone wants to be loved. Dakota didn't feel loved. Peggy went on to learn and play the guitar without her companion, Kid Dakota, alongside her.

Not long after Dakota gave up guitar lessons, a lady friend of Mom's from the school PTA came over to Dakota's home. She was sitting and talking with Mom in the living room. She motioned to Dakota like she wanted to ask him something. "Dakota, would you be willing to learn a song and sing it at the school Christmas show?" With a big smile, Dakota excitedly replied, "Yes. Yes!" The lady was tickled and told Dakota, "I'll be your teacher. I'll teach you a song to sing at the Christmas show."

Dakota now had a sparkle back as he learned to sing and then performed the song flawlessly at the Christmas show. Dakota got what he needed: a standing ovation. The audience loved him. Dakota was trying to find some solid footing and the applause was the medicine he needed. They liked the Kid Dakota. The boy was successful—that was good, real good.

This youngster was learning how to overcome abuses that had unjustly come his way even though hurtful remarks didn't bounce off him like a rubber ball. They stung each and every time. Dakota needed to build remarkable inner strength, with the strength of steel, to forge his way and eventually to mold and shape him who he would become. His smile, humor and determination continued to shine through his own personal darkness, turning the darkness into light around him.

The next few years would prove to be even more challenging for Dakota as he kept looking for the pot of gold buried under the avalanche of his extraordinary personal difficulties.

FIVE

Moving Forward

Grammar school parents and kids

Dakota loved to learn new things. He liked sports and at his sports-focused grammar school they had father-son baseball games the kids enjoyed. Sports included learning to square dance to the western music he liked. Square dancing during the late '40s and early '50s was very popular with the kids and teachers as well. Dakota liked to have fun. He enjoyed hanging out with girls just as much as the guys; he was popular with both.

Dakota wasn't considered a smart student. He always struggled to maintain average grades. For Dakota, reading and concentration were particularly difficult. Dakota was haunted by gender confusion, which affected his ability to stay focused.

Even in all of that, Dakota enjoyed being funny to help overcome the darkness inside of him. All the kids loved him because he was a funny guy. Dakota could make people laugh even when they shouldn't be laughing.

With Papa's passion for camping, it was no surprise that he encouraged his older boy, Danny, when he was old enough, to join the local Boy Scout troop. The scouts were always doing something fun outdoors. Papa and Danny quickly took to the scouting traditions of camping and hiking and all the opportunities scouting offered. Danny was smart, so with Papa's encouragement Danny quickly ascended through each level in scouting. Starting with tenderfoot, then second class, he was on his way. Danny did all this before Dakota was old enough to join the scouts.

One day, Papa told Dakota, "You know you're old enough now. I think joining the Boy Scouts would be great for you." Dakota had no problem jumping at the chance. He was tired of sitting at home while Papa and Danny went to scouting events. Papa was happy; both of his boys were in the Boy Scouts. No underachiever himself, Papa became very involved in leadership in the local troop so he could be with his boys. Papa eventually became the Area District Commissioner for the organization whose slogan was "God and our country."

The sponsor for their troop was a local independent bottled water company which lent the troop its large trucks with their drivers for the monthly scouting events. Thirty to forty kids would go camping and hiking in the southern California mountains. Thanks to the company's support, the entire troop went to the very first Scout Jamboree ever held in California. Scout troops from all over the United States and other countries gathered for about five days and enjoyed learning camping and life skills, such as chopping wood, surviving in the wilderness, starting a campfire without matches, and building an emergency shelter.

But not one person ever suspected how much Dakota's smiles and humor covered his shame and darkness. The desire for the dress didn't go away that day when Papa swiftly made it disappear. Dakota only wished it were that easy. The truth was Dakota never stopped struggling because thoughts about the dress were like a neighbor who won't stop knocking on the door. Now at twelve years of age the kid was mired in silent shame, holding on to the feelings that Nana and her dress-up game set off inside him.

Oh, how the kid enjoyed the scouting events and the overnight camping in the fresh California mountain air with a sky filled with a million stars. One night Dakota was lying on his back staring with complete amazement at the stars that lit up the pitch black sky. He silently asked for a star to light up his darkness. But that star wouldn't come to Dakota this night. The kid went into his single man pup tent and curled up in his sleeping bag for a night's sleep. He didn't know he was about to encounter something he never bargained for.

This weekend was like most of the other camping trips with the scouts into the California foothills. Each boy slept in the privacy of his own small, one-man pup tent. Dakota was sleeping the cold night away, snug in his sleeping bag, when he suddenly was awakened, startled by an unfamiliar voice whispering, "Dakota, are you awake?"

As Dakota cleared the sleep from his eyes, he could see the head of a boy sticking partly inside the tent. Looking directly at this unfamiliar head, Dakota whispered in return, "Who are you? What are you doing?" The voice responded, "It's Byron, but you can call me Bi." Dakota was now fully awake and didn't like the sound of this. He said to the unwanted intruder in a stern voice, "What the heck do you want?" Byron moved further inside the tiny pup tent. Dakota wasn't whispering this time when he spoke, "Get out of here. Go back to your own tent." Byron whispered back, "I want to corn hole you." Dakota loudly replied, "I don't know what that is and I want to sleep, so go away. Get out of my tent."

It was over. Byron made a quick retreat from Dakota's tent. Thankfully, nothing took place that night except an exchange of words. Byron was a tall kid and heavy for his age. Was this just another unwanted encounter because Kid Dakota was small for his age and people young and old assumed he couldn't easily defend himself? The next day Byron and Dakota acted as if it never happened. No further words were spoken between them about Byron's visit to Dakota's tent in the darkness.

The weekend camping trip was over, and the scout troop broke camp and headed home. At home, Papa and his boys went their separate ways to unpack their bags. Dakota finished and joined his dad in the living room. "Dakota, did you enjoy the weekend away?" Dakota responded, "Yes, it was great fun. But, Papa, do you know the big boy named Byron?" Papa replied, "Yes, he's new in scouts. It was his first trip. Why do you ask?" Dakota shyly responded, "Well, he woke me up in the middle of the night and came inside my pup tent. He whispered that he wanted to corn hole me."

Papa snapped his head around in shock. "Tell me again what he said." Dakota said it a second time, "He said he wanted to corn hole me." Papa's face was red with anger as he asked, "Did Byron touch you?" Dakota quickly responded, "No, no, Papa. I told him to go away and he did." Dakota wasn't sure if he should be concerned; he didn't know what corn hole was. But the look on Papa's face told Dakota it was something bad.

Papa pressed Dakota a second time, "Did this really happen or did you make this up? I want the truth." It was clear Papa had his doubts about the story. Papa was the troop scoutmaster at the time, responsible not for just his own boys but for all the scouts in the troop. Papa's role was to protect all the kids on the weekend camping trips and he took his responsibility seriously. He knew he would need to talk to Byron's mom and he wanted to make sure he had the facts straight first.

Dakota, in his most convincing, strong voice, said "Yes, Papa, it really did happen. It's the truth, but it's no big deal, is it?" Papa didn't respond to the "no big deal" question. What happened next surprised Dakota. Papa said something his youngest son rarely heard from his beloved papa, "I believe you, Dakota."

It must have been an hour or more before Papa came home. Dakota came into the living room as Papa was sharing bits of the conversation with Mom Ellie. "Bryon's mother told me her son has had problems with approaching boys this way and she thought scouting would help him." Papa turned toward Dakota and his posture was calm, "You won't see Byron anymore on weekend trips. His mom doesn't want to hear any more reports like this." Dakota still wasn't sure what corn hole was until he asked a buddy of his at school. Then he knew why Byron wouldn't be back in scouting for any more overnight weekends.

The scouts gave Papa and his boys some great memories; the incident with Byron didn't steal any of the joy of scouting from Dakota. When Papa realized how much his boys enjoyed camping, he went all out and purchased new gear: a Coleman stove, lanterns, a big tent, table and chairs, so the family could get out in the fresh air and enjoy the outdoors together. From the California gold country to the national parks, Dakota and Danny thoroughly enjoyed the special vacation road trips the four of them took in the old V8 Ford. All were really good memories; great times for Kid Dakota and his older brother, Danny.

Dakota was promoted from grammar school to the local junior high school, following in his brother's footsteps a year before. But this kid couldn't escape thinking he would have been better off if he were born a girl. Thanks to Nana, the memory of playing the dress-up game was like a radio stuck in the "on" position in his head repeating the phrase, "You should've been a girl." There was no "off" position.

Dakota found a way to indulge and expand his fun-loving nature in a theater arts class, a place where he could express his sense of humor. Dakota excelled in drama, performing playful skits at the "Noon Theater." He loved the stage. Dakota was so good he was asked to join the school's performing arts team. He memorized Hamlet's third soliloquy, "To be or not to be" for competition. Dakota's drama coach encouraged him to interpret the piece as Hamlet would: whether to live or not to live, and whether or not to commit suicide. The kid achieved high marks for his performances.

Brother Danny joined the "B" lightweight division football team. Danny was slightly bigger than Dakota but still small enough for the "B" team. Danny had a lot of brains. He could read for hours on end but he didn't have much athletic ability. The proof of this came the very first day of full contact football practice. Danny was trying to tackle someone and he broke his arm. Danny never went back to football. He decided reading books was safer.

When Dakota's time came to join the "B" football team he was one of the lightest and smallest kids on the team. He got knocked around by the other kids in practice like he was a rubber ball. He got creamed every time. Blocking and tackling were a disaster. But the kid had something the other kids didn't have: a great kicking leg. The coaches saw Dakota could kick better than anyone else on the team so he became the team kicker.

As that damn dress continued to occupy permanent residence in his head, Dakota made every effort to push it aside. This kid just kept going forward, no matter what. In his early teens he decided he wanted to start making some money. He had some ideas and he needed to talk with Papa. One Saturday morning, at the same table where all hell had broken loose over the "dress in the drawer" years before, Dakota turned to Papa and stood before him with the posture of an up-and-coming CEO.

"Papa, can I use your lawnmower so I can start cutting lawns and earning money?"

That got Papa to smile, even chuckle, "Sure you can, but you know a lawn mower isn't easy to push and the people will want you do a real good job."

Dakota, looking like he knew it all, said, "Sure, Papa, I'll do great. I know that."

Papa stood up from the table, motioned to his little guy and said, "Come with me." To the garage they went; Dakota following Papa. "Come on, young man. We'll get the lawnmower out. Try pushing it."

Papa stood by, observing his boy. The kid grabbed the mower handle and pushed the lawnmower with a big burst forward. The kid was running behind the mower, being a real show-off trying to impress Papa. He turned toward Papa for approval. Papa was enjoying Dakota so much he was laughing his head off. With obvious joy and pride in his younger son, Papa said, "You'll do fine. Just go for it. Use the lawnmower all you want. Go earn some money, but save some, too."

Dakota went knocking on neighbors' doors pitching his lawn service. Two out of ten said yes so he was now in business for himself. This determined kid grew his business to the point where Papa had to drive him to homes that were several blocks away with the lawnmower and rakes in the car trunk. If someone had uncut grass this kid was knocking on the door. "I can cut your grass once a week for a dollar." He got more jobs.

But he wasn't about to stop with cutting lawns. When he discovered he could earn some money delivering the morning newspaper, he was all in. Every Thursday at 5 a.m. he walked with a big white bag fitted over his shoulders full of newspapers. Folding newspapers as he walked, Kid Dakota delivered the Los Angeles weekly to every home on his route. Then he found an afternoon route with another newspaper for six days a week to sixty homes. This kid now had three different jobs earning money. But even at that, he couldn't stop the radio in his head playing all the dress chatter. It just wouldn't stop.

For the afternoon paper route Dakota needed to use his bicycle. The newspaper provided special canvas bags that were made to hang over the rear fender. Each side held about fifteen papers, about thirty newspapers at a time. His route had sixty home deliveries so the area coordinator who provided the newspapers set up two drop locations with thirty papers at each location. Dakota's legs got stronger as he peddled the bike with the load of heavy newspapers.

Collecting payments taught this young entrepreneur the value of charming people with his wit to earn tips. Dakota was raking in a whopping sixty dollars a month delivering newspapers. He had his walking route every Thursday morning and his bicycle route six afternoons a week. Together with proceeds from his lawn cutting business, this kid was building a real bank, at least in his sock drawer.

The fad among the kids had been iridescent colored socks. Everybody had the bright colored socks that looked like they could glow in the dark. But like all fads, this one, too, faded as quickly as it came. Dakota used the unpopular socks as his bank. He stuffed all his earnings, paper and coin, into the socks; not neatly, he just jammed the money in there. Dakota thought if Mom found the money in the dresser drawer it wouldn't cause a shock wave through the house like the dress did.

All of Dakota's hard work, unfortunately, did nothing to eliminate his obsessive thoughts about dressing like a girl. His desire to dress in girl's clothes just wouldn't go away, no matter what Dakota did. It was like he was born that way. His desires always got the best of him. When he delivered newspapers he looked for discarded girl's clothing in trashcans. He felt bad but he couldn't stop himself. When he found female clothing in the trash, he grabbed it and hid it inside his canvas bags. He eventually scored another dress which wasn't too badly soiled. He took the newly discovered goods home where he made sure to hide them in the garage rafters, not in his dresser drawer. Dakota felt some shame that he couldn't halt his feelings.

Scavenging in the trash cans, Dakota struck pay dirt several times and cobbled together a wardrobe of women's clothing. The dress-up game Nana had started remained alive and was now an obsession. In fact, the feelings became even more intense over time. The kid wasn't a homosexual. For him the question was: "Am I a boy or am I a girl?" He felt one way and looked another.

Dakota functioned well as a boy. He always had girlfriends, like Bobbette, a cute redhead from school. Dakota's buddies wondered: How did he attract all the good looking gals? Dakota's secret weapons were his endearing humor, big smile and playful nature.

Dakota always wanted to make more money. Off he went again, looking for a job at a local gas station long before he even could drive a car. He landed a job at the gas station located on the main intersection in town, just a few blocks from his home, for twenty-five cents an hour. The owner was a crotchety old goat of a man who never said anything nice to anyone. Dakota's coworker was a real cool guy named Vic who was a student at a college just down the street from the station. Vic got the kid a raise to fifty cents because he was good with the customers. Dakota never sat around; he couldn't sit quietly. He always kept busy cleaning the lube rack, stacking old tires and helping customers. Dakota's papa said many times to his boy, "Whatever you do, make sure to leave a place in better shape because you were there, even if you are only there for a day."

This growing youngster was a cool, fun-loving kid whom everyone liked, except for his brother, but brothers never like each other, right? His older brother, Danny, had no desire to cut lawns or deliver newspapers and wasn't motivated by earning money.

Dakota carried around his secret with the dress-up game. It was all his and his only now. When Nana played the dress-up game, she made the dress for him. Now Dakota found girl's clothing in the trash and secretly stored it in the garage. The troubled kid even came up with the female name, Crystal West, who became the replacement for his imaginary buddy, Coach. Dakota hadn't conferred with Coach for a long time.

Dakota, at thirteen or so years old, knew the female feelings were never going away, no matter what. If he could have gotten them to go away, he would have by now. Visualizing himself in female dress was now a permanent part of his dreams and thoughts. Who knew that the game Nana started at her house would become unstoppable? Dakota had developed a deep dislike for Nana, feeling like she really had hurt him.

In his early teen years, Dakota continued to enjoy drama class and excelled in theater arts. Each year, his school competed with twenty-five or so others in a three-day event for a host of awards such as best play, best actor and best supporting actor. The venue for the competition was The Pasadena Playhouse, a well-known popular venue for plays, where Hollywood actors often headlined in order to sharpen their skills and they served on the panel of judges for the school competitions.

Dakota was cast as the kid Harvey in a little-known play entitled *The All American Ape*. Harvey was a major character and appeared in all three acts of the play. For Dakota, the highlight was the last scene of the last act of the play. Alone on the stage, Harvey needed to hold the audience's attention all the way to the closing of the curtain without saying one word, just using emotion and stage movement.

The scene opened with the kid Harvey knocking on his neighbor's door: knock, knock, knock. Harvey idolized his neighbor, an all-American football player nicknamed the All American Ape. Dakota, playing his part very well, kept knocking on the door, but the football player didn't answer. Harvey slowly turned the door handle. Holding the audience in suspense, he pushed tentatively on the door and peeked through the opening. Seeing the room was empty, Harvey walked in.

The window of the third-story flat was open. The curtains hanging from the window were blowing outward with the wind. Harvey walked over to the window. Looking down toward the ground, he started to cry. Then the audience realized the football player had jumped to his death. Dakota needed to convey to the audience his reaction to finding the All American Ape on the ground, dead. Harvey, crying, turned his back to the window and, with a great theatrical "double take," looked up at the fireplace mantle on the opposite wall The All American Ape's game ball rested atop the mantle above the fireplace. This special game ball was given to the All American at the end of his last game. From the time Harvey had first knocked on the door, not a word had been spoken. Harvey slid a chair over to the fireplace to climb up and stand on. All the time, Harvey was crying. He stretched out his arms to reach that special game ball. Holding the ball in his arms like it was a baby, Harvey turned toward the audience weeping as the curtain slowly closed. That was "The End." The audience went wild with approval. Dakota garnered the second highest scores for a supporting actor in the three days of competition. Not bad for a kid whose mind held secrets of shame and whose sock drawer held old socks stuffed with money.

The kid was talented. Dakota was good at most anything he did, from delivering newspapers and cutting grass to theater arts. Dakota knew he could never excel like his older brother when it came to reading or getting good grades, but he kept looking for his own niche. He built up a good kicking leg by pedaling his bike loaded with newspapers. Both legs were strong. After "B" football season ended, Dakota wanted to try running on the school track team. Track was popular for outgoing competitive kids like Dakota who weren't afraid to fail. Our kid was just perfect for the track team.

By this time Dakota was no longer a fat "butterball." Playing football, mowing lawns and pumping the pedals on his bike loaded with newspapers had worked him down to a slim one hundred and twenty-seven pounds, a nice weight for his small frame.

Dakota was a good buddy, the kind of kid who had a lot of friends including the smart students and great athletes; they all liked Dakota. But being small for his age made him a target for bullies to push around and mess with. Two guys would grab Dakota by his arms and push him into the girls' bathroom. The big guys liked to taunt him because they knew he wouldn't fight back.

One of Dakota's friends, Larry, was the first-string quarterback for the "A" heavyweight football team. Kid Dakota had been friends with this big guy all the way back in second grade at grammar school. Larry was known to be tough and Larry hated guys who picked on guys smaller than themselves.

They wouldn't have a chance in a fight with Larry. He didn't mind messing them up. Larry made sure the bullies knew his friend, Dakota, was "off limits." He told them, "If you want to mess with Dakota, you'll need to mess with me first." That ended the bullying of Dakota.

Dakota started to dream about cars and how much money he would need to purchase one that he really liked. He needed to find a job that brought in more money. He got lucky. During a family event he made a connection with the owner of a small automotive repair shop in the next town. This shop was the place for tune-ups, brakes and electrical repair. The man's name was Eric. When Dakota approached him about working for him, Eric told Dakota on the spot, "You've got the job. Just come to the shop and start helping to keep the brake shop clean, empty the trash, and sweep the floor. Keep the place spotless." Dakota was so excited. It was his first real job, more than working at a gas station, delivering papers or cutting grass. He didn't even ask about how much money; he didn't even care. He had a real job! He could drop the paper routes and work at the automotive shop as many hours as Eric would allow.

Dakota was fifteen years old, not old enough to drive so the big Monarch road bike that was his newspaper delivery machine became his transportation to the auto repair shop three miles away. To start, his schedule was Saturdays until school let out for the summer and then six days a week during the summer months.

The first summer, Kid Dakota worked fifty hours a week. In the early light of the summer sun this kid mounted his bike and rode to the shop. In the fall, Dakota worked Saturdays as he attended high school. He loved working at the auto shop and continued to work there the following summer, too.

Dakota worked so he could fill his iridescent socks, the makeshift bank in his dresser drawer, with even more of that cash. The kid had saved lots of money through the years. Now just weeks shy of his sixteenth birthday, he was ready to spend a little on his first car. He wanted a real hot rod but he thought that would come later. Dakota found a 1950 Oldsmobile with V8 power and automatic transmission. He had learned about automatic transmissions from working at the automobile shop. Most cars of the day had a manual transmission with a clutch. Dakota wanted automatic transmission because it could shift faster and easier than a stick shift.

Dakota passed his driver's education class at school, got his driver's license and purchased his first car, that 1950 V8 Oldsmobile. That old '50 Oldsmobile was a green four-door, the same color as his papa's old '41 Ford. It burned almost as much oil as it did gas: about a quart of oil every hundred miles, a sure sign the engine wasn't so fresh and new. But Dakota didn't care. Driving was the goal. To Dakota, the Olds was just a temporary ride until he saved some more money.

Having a car and a driver's license changed Dakota's world. With a car, Dakota could drive to the automotive shop after school. He no longer needed his well-worn, heavy Monarch bike for transportation. With a driver's license in hand, Dakota was tapped by the shop owner, Eric, to drive the parts delivery truck. Dakota was now the parts delivery guy.

One Saturday while Dakota was out making deliveries, he pulled into the driveway of his next stop, a paint and body shop. Dakota looked up and found himself looking directly at a fabulous 1934 Ford hot rod. This Ford was amazing: a two-door with a "chopped top" and a magnificent reddish root beer paint color. Dakota had just found his first love in this car. The 1934 Ford sported a "for sale" sign in the window. Dakota smiled real big as he remembered all the cash he had stuffed into the socks. Would he have enough money? Were all his years of hard work about to pay off?

For a moment, Dakota was so star-struck he forgot he was there to deliver parts. Now he was on a mission to find out if he had enough money to purchase this amazing hot rod. The sign said the '34 Ford had a 1950 Oldsmobile V8 engine tucked under the hood. Dakota knew the power of that Olds V8. With his CEO mindset and strut, Dakota walked up to the man who was working on another car in the shop and boldly asked, "Is that red '34 really for sale?"

The man turned around so he was face to face with the teenager and said, "Yes, it is, but it ain't cheap. And it'll be 'nother month 'til I finish the work on it." Dakota's smile got bigger as he asked, "How much ya asking for it?" The man looked at this young kid as if this hot rod was out of his league and firmly stated, "$1,200. It has 45 hand-rubbed coats of mandarin red lacquer paint, a fresh V8 engine, all new 'tuck and roll' leather seats and new tires." Without any hesitation Dakota replied, "Will ya take $1,000 cash money? I can have it here tomorrow." The man chuckled under his breath as he looked at the brash boy because a thousand bucks in 1957 was big money. But this guy didn't know this kid. The man asked, "Where are you goin' ta get that much money?" Dakota quickly noticed the man didn't say no to his offer of $1,000.

Dakota went on to tell him he had been saving his earnings for years and only spent a little bit on the old Oldsmobile he was driving, "I got the money in my sock drawer." With that, the man laughed out loud. Dakota could see the man had great admiration for his spunk and skills in negotiation. The man said with a smile, "If you can bring me the $1,000 tomorrow by 5 p.m., it's yours."

No ground under Kid Dakota's feet—he was flying high as he pumped his right arm upward in a victory celebration. He knew he had the money. "Thank you, thank you," Dakota exclaimed, over and over because he knew he would have the best looking car of anyone in high school. This kid had accomplished everything he set his sights on from the time he first pushed that lawn mower in his backyard. This was a good day.

Dakota moved from being a kid to a young man in a bold flash. He was a working youngster who wasn't yet out of high school. He still had all the junk inside his head. The girl and the dress wouldn't go away. But even so, he had some great moments and this was definitely a great moment.

Dakota was giddy with excitement as he finally delivered the car parts he had brought. He completed his work that day and upon arriving at home he told Papa the good news: he was going to purchase a 1934 Ford not far from home. Papa was apprehensive. Did Dakota have the skill or ability to evaluate a good car purchase? After all, one thousand dollars was a massive amount of money. Papa wanted to protect his son so he kindly suggested, "Let's drive over right now and look at the car before you give him the money tomorrow." So, Papa and the boy went off to the shop to see the car.

During the short drive, Dakota talked a mile a minute, giving his sales pitch to Papa about how great the '34 Ford was: the paint job, the engine and the new tires. He assured Papa that he had all the money he needed to pay for it.

The '34 Ford was sitting outside where Dakota had first laid eyes on it. Dakota shouted, "There's the car—the red one." As Papa turned slowly into the driveway and spied the Ford, his eyes popped.

"It's the red car?"

"Yep, Papa. That's it and I've got the money."

Papa stared in complete amazement.

"It is absolutely beautiful! No wonder you want it. Do you really have enough money for that car?"

"More than enough, Papa."

This display of his kid's spunk and mature eye had stunned Papa to silence. Kid Dakota, who earlier in the day had gained the respect of a stranger and negotiated to buy a car, now made his papa stand up and take notice. Papa looked admiringly at his boy, suddenly looking grown up. Dakota, not smart at school work, had just demonstrated his talent for working, earning money and saving with a purpose. His laser focus allowed him to purchase a great car. Papa thought it was fabulous that all of Dakota's efforts to earn and save money had paid nice dividends. Papa was happy and that was very important to the kid.

Dakota, on the outside, was this amazing guy, an incredible kid who got that '34 Ford hot rod because he worked hard to get it. Inside, a war raged every day over his desire to dress up and even become a female. Dakota was a great kid with two sides: able to achieve great success, yet with a shameful secret—an unwavering desire to see himself undergo a surgical gender change.

At school, Dakota's friends were so excited about his hot rod that they assigned him a special parking place. They insisted that his car take the number one slot next to the athletic gymnasium, a parking space that showed off the car.

High school was going well. Dakota was just a great kid. He had three girlfriends. He and his hot rod Ford were in a school car club. He ran on the track team. He remained active in theater arts performing in lunch hour short plays.

Dakota's grades were nowhere near the top of his class but he graduated from high school, the very same school from which his papa graduated thirty-five years prior. After graduation he and his classmates scattered in all directions. Dakota continued to work at the automotive shop. Because of his performance in the play, *The All American Ape*, Dakota was invited to audition at the famous Pasadena Playhouse.

Dakota was discovering he could do almost anything he made up his mind to do. But unfortunately, life would throw him some curveballs that placed that into question. One day all was well; the next, not so good.

SIX

After Graduation

Dakota's prized '34 Ford

Dakota's performance as Harvey in *The All American Ape* attracted the attention of a Hollywood casting director who was in the audience. He contacted Dakota through the school to invite the kid to audition for a part. But like so often happens, a simple event derailed Dakota's opportunity.

The day before the audition the axle on Dakota's '34 Ford hot rod broke as he was driving about one mile from home. The car was unable to move. Dakota knocked on the door of the nearest house and asked the home owner to call the Auto Club for a tow.

The tow truck driver who arrived wasn't the brightest bulb in the chandelier; in fact, his next actions proved he was inept.

When the tow truck driver hooked up the chains to the hot rod to get it into position to tow, instead of hooking the chains to the frame of the car, he wrapped them around the car's flimsy back bumper. As the driver hoisted the car up by its bumper, he did extensive damage to the rear area of the '34 Ford. A tow was supposed to move damaged cars, not damage cars that needed a tow. The driver was a knucklehead, for sure.

Dakota uncharacteristically exploded in anger. He stomped around, repeating very loudly, "How dumb can you get; how utterly stupid?!" Dakota couldn't grasp how a tow truck driver, someone who towed cars every day for a living, couldn't anticipate that he would damage the car by attaching the chains to the bumper instead of to the frame. Dakota grew up with a tow truck driver, Grandpa "Stumpy." Dakota told the careless tow truck driver, "My grandpa would never attempt to tow a car that way."

Finally, the '34 Ford, with a broken axle and looking so sad with unnecessary body damage, was hooked up by its rear end properly to be towed. Dakota rode with the driver in the cab of the tow truck. He knew the axle wasn't going to take much work, but the body work—that was another story. Dakota was firm with the driver, "You'll be responsible for repairing the body and paint, and the repairs will be done by the guy who built the car and did the original paint and bodywork." The tow truck driver had an answer, "We aren't responsible. There is a clause on the tow release form you signed. It reads we are not responsible for damage."

Dakota was boiling over with anger.

"We'll see about that. The form says accidental damage. What you did to my car was no accident. It was stupid and you'll pay for it."

The driver dropped the '34 Ford on the grounds of the towing office. He was pissed off. He pointed his finger at Dakota and said, "You're nothing but a little punk."

Dakota turned his back on the guy and stomped into the towing office. He grabbed the first phone he could find and called his papa for a ride home. He let Papa know what happened. When Papa arrived, he told the Auto Club tow driver, "Don't touch the car until I get back to you about this."

The next day, with no other car, Dakota had no way to get to the audition and he blew the audition off. They were none too happy and told him no second chance would come. Dakota just wanted to get the '34 Ford repaired. The hot rod was more important than the audition as far as Dakota was concerned.

Papa had been a longtime member of the Auto Club so he went downtown to the main office to file a complaint and swift action took place. The Auto Club representative assured Papa that the tow company's contract with the Auto Club would be terminated by the end of the month. Then he told Papa to take the '34 to any shop he wanted. "Get your son's car repaired. The Auto Club will pay all the costs." Papa was Dakota's hero. Papa modeled how to resolve a problem without a fight, although the kid did want to punch the tow truck driver just so he would feel better.

Kid Dakota, high school graduate, was on the hunt for a new career. Working at the automotive repair shop felt like a dead end. Dakota wanted to expand his employment opportunities. The aerospace industry was new and growing, with drafting jobs available. Dakota enjoyed his drafting class in high school so he thought, "I could do that. Why not try for one of the drafting jobs? I need a little more schooling first, but I'm going do it."

Dakota enrolled in a local city college drafting class and did very well in the class. As a result of his good grades and presenting himself well in interviews, the unstoppable nineteen year old landed a good job at a large aerospace firm. Dakota loved his work as a draftsman. His responsibilities included preparing electrical schematics and printed circuit board drawings at a drafting table. All in all, this was much better than being in a dirty car repair shop all day.

This was the year 1959. Television shows like *Bonanza* and *Rawhide* were popular. Television sets back then were small and stuffed inside a decorative console cabinet about thirty inches high and several feet long. They reminded Dakota of the little radios of the 1940s that were housed inside a three foot tall art deco box. Fifties music reigned supreme with talents like Elvis Presley, Connie Francis, Paul Anka and Ritchie Valens, and groups such as The Everly Brothers, The Coasters and The Platters. A new group called Tom and Jerry had a minor hit with "Hey, Schoolgirl" and within a few years they developed a signature sound and renamed themselves Simon and Garfunkel.

Dakota loved his '34 Ford but to keep it in good condition, it needed to be kept in a garage that he didn't have—he was living at home. It wasn't a road car; it was a hot rod and Dakota wanted a car that he could drive long distances. He found a 1955 Chevy that he could restore to replace the '34 Ford.

One afternoon Dakota was hanging out with a neighbor friend who was talking about his psychology studies at a local university and the stories his professor told about people who needed psychological help. This touched a nerve in Dakota. Some of the stories sounded something like his and like the dress obsession he couldn't get out of his head. Dakota encouraged his friend to tell him more of the stories. The psychology student described several mental issues before getting to the topic of obsessions. "Yeah," he told Dakota, "People get obsessed with all kinds of things. They can't stop and they need help to quit." Dakota knew then what Nana did to him must have caused his obsession with the dress; at least Dakota suspected that could be his problem.

Dakota asked his friend, "What's your professor's name?"

"Father Caldwell. Why do you want to know?"

"Just curious."

Within a few days Dakota called the Catholic university, asked for Father Caldwell and was connected to the professor's office. Dakota told him why he was calling.

"I was talking to one of your students and wanted to know if you do private counseling?"

"Yes, I do. Are you a student here at the university?"

"No, I work as a draftsman. My friend, the student in your class, is unaware I'm calling you."

"That's fine. I have time every Saturday at 10 a.m. Can you come this Saturday?"

Dakota was delighted and said, "Yes, I can come this Saturday. Let's do that. Where is your office?" With that, Dakota decided to start getting help for his gender change obsession.

Getting psychological help was Dakota's idea. Dakota felt Nana's actions did him damage and he longed to be free from the obsession. Dakota didn't want his parents to know about the therapy—another secret he would keep to himself. Dakota didn't like keeping secrets from his parents, but he felt he needed to hide that he was seeking therapy because they didn't know the dress game had never ended.

The next Saturday Dakota joined the professor in his office for his 10 o'clock appointment. After a few minutes of introductions Caldwell asked when Dakota first started dressing in girl's clothes. Dakota wasn't all that comfortable but explained anyway.

"It all started at my nana's house at the age of four."

"How often did the dressing up in girl's clothes take place?"

The kid, still not comfortable, answered, "Every time I stayed over on weekends and I was alone with her. It happened a lot."

"Did you encourage your grandma to dress you in girl's clothes?"

Dakota, feeling uncertain, said in a sheepish kind of tone, "I don't really know. I didn't feel like I could stop her from dressing me that way."

The professor made a suggestion: "I think you need to start writing down in a journal what your feelings are during the time you are dressing in girl's clothes."

Dakota was shocked. "Really? That's going be hard to do. I'm living at home and I don't have the privacy to dress up. I was hoping you'd help me stop dressing."

The professor replied, "I don't think you have control over your dressing. We need to explore what's driving you to dress in female clothing now."

"Okay, but I'm not sure what you want me to do."

Caldwell explained, "Just write down on lined paper what you're feeling and if you feel there is a trigger that sets the desire in motion."

Dakota nodded and said, "I can do that."

They talked more, even talking about how Kid Dakota listened to sounds to escape his feelings.

Soon the counseling session was over. With a deep breath, Dakota walked back to his car in the university parking lot and pointed the car toward home. He had completed the first counseling he had ever had and it came fifteen years after Nana started dressing him in girl's clothes. It seemed to him that the counselor's suggestion wasn't going to prevent him from dressing but encouraging him because he would be looking for the triggers and feelings. "That's not the way to stop all this," Dakota thought.

To comply with Father Caldwell's request to dress in female clothing and then write about his feelings would require some guarantee of privacy. It was clear that living at home with Papa and Mom would no longer be possible. It didn't offer enough privacy. Dakota knew he needed to move out and live on his own. He had known the day to move out would come someday. His older brother Danny had already moved out, gotten married and wasn't living at home. It was Dakota's turn.

Moving out wouldn't set so well with Papa or Mom, for sure. Dakota felt pain knowing all that was going on was the direct result of the damn dress-up game Nana started. Now the negative impact of her influence was piling up on him: the need for therapy, the need to move out, and the shame of dressing in female clothing. The obsession was as much depressing as it was so damn confusing.

Within a few days Dakota found a furnished apartment near his work for only sixty-five dollars a month. It was only a few miles from his parents' home. With the new apartment came new neighbors. Next door to Dakota was Chuck Ahʻo, an outgoing guy from Hawaii who liked his beer. From Chuck, the kid would learn to master the art of nightly beer busts. Adding alcohol to cross-dressing was a volatile cocktail for Dakota, not good therapy. The daily drinking became the new trigger to dress in female clothing instead of the feelings he was supposed to write about for the psychologist. The sessions with Father Caldwell ended as quickly as they started. Dakota didn't like the idea of engaging in cross-dressing as therapy to end cross-dressing.

Dakota's skills at drafting made his work days great. He enjoyed the people with whom he worked and aerospace was the up-and-coming place to be. But this young man had an unquenchable thirst to always improve and grow; perhaps it was another obsession. He always wanted more. Dakota had his eye on another, much larger aerospace company about forty miles away in Orange County, southeast of L.A., which employed about 100,000 people. His brother, Danny, worked there as an engineer. But Dakota's career move would have to wait.

Papa needed help. Papa, who owned and operated his own small industrial belting manufacturing company, needed his young son to come in and help him. Papa had been a smoker of unfiltered cigarettes from the age of fourteen. Now in his mid-forties, he had been diagnosed with lung cancer and wasn't feeling well at all. He was struggling. His strength was failing and he needed his young son to do some of the work he couldn't do. When Dakota looked at Papa he could see the illness which had invaded the body of this 180-pound man, consuming him day by day. The cancer was cutting his papa down painfully and relentlessly. It was difficult for Dakota to witness his papa fading away right before his eyes and it became yet another blow in his young life.

Dakota put aside his drafting position for now and went to work for his papa, but only for a short time. Papa wanted Dakota's hands on the daily work just to keep his business alive. But Dakota found he didn't have the skills or abilities Papa needed. Even so, Dakota knew this would become the most special time he ever spent with his papa whom he really loved.

It was awful for Dakota to see his great papa so damn sick and failing. Papa tried everything he could to teach Dakota the necessary skills to hold on to the business. But more important to Dakota was just being there with his papa. They were side by side, papa and son; nothing could be better than that. The illness was killing Papa and with him, the business he had built from scratch. The financial picture was grim. Papa needed to file for bankruptcy. The best efforts of young Dakota just couldn't pull off the saving of the business.

Papa told Dakota that he felt Dakota had done everything he could and that it was time to move on. "Go; get the drafting position at the aerospace company where your brother works." Danny worked in the engineering department and gave Dakota's resume to an engineer who needed someone like Dakota as part of his expanding drafting group. The initial opportunity was given because his brother opened the door and then Dakota landed the job on the strength of his previous work history and his schooling.

Dakota rented a room in a house near work and walked thirty minutes through the orange groves to his office. At the new job, Dakota performed many of the same tasks he had done previously, such as drafting drawings for printed circuit boards and electrical schematics. After Papa's bankruptcy, Mom and Papa needed some help with the home finances and Dakota did what he could. Dakota sold his restored '55 Chevy, leaving him to ride the Greyhound bus to come home to help on the weekends, a forty-mile trip from Orange County.

After only a few weeks, Dakota's dad was no longer able to even walk. The cancer had attacked his bones, especially in his back and he was losing weight fast. Mom Ellie had been a trouper caring for Papa but now she needed Kid Dakota's help at home during the week, too. His big brother was married and living forty miles away, so it was up to the kid to help care for Papa. Mom rented a hospital bed to make Papa comfortable and Dakota moved back home to help. Now he needed a good commuting car to get to work. Somehow through the generosity of friends, Mom cobbled together the down payment for him to purchase a new, fuel saving, thirty-two miles per gallon Volvo 122S two door.

Even though Mom and Dakota were working, money was tight. Paying for twenty-four-hour nursing care wasn't an option. Dakota and Mom Ellie devised a plan so that one of them was always with Papa, day and night. They took alternating night shifts. Mom Ellie stayed up all night with Papa while Dakota slept. Then the following night, Dakota stayed up all night to be with Papa so Mom could sleep. Someone was always there so Papa wouldn't feel abandoned or alone.

Papa's pain intensified and he required morphine injections just to get a bit of relief. Papa was so ill and medicated that his words made no sense and he couldn't put a sentence together. But Papa loved his boys and his wife. Brother Danny came to visit, if only to hold Papa's hand and smile. No matter what had occurred prior to this, the love of each family member for the others was unmistakable.

For Dakota, working full-time, driving forty miles each way to work, missing every other night of sleep, and dealing with the deep emotional pain of a dying papa, were taking a toll. After a few weeks it became noticeable to Dakota's boss something was wrong. Dakota had a great working relationship with the boss, a very smart engineer with a great name: Katsumi Wakamatsu. He requested everyone just call him "Elmer." Elmer was one of the nicest guys Dakota had ever known. Elmer was a brilliant guy who had a heart for people. He was always kind and encouraging to everyone. Elmer noticed the kid was tired and depressed; not his usual exuberant self with the big smile and quick sense of humor. Elmer didn't know Dakota's pop was dying from cancer and that Dakota had moved home to help care for him, commuting forty miles each way every day, and staying up all night every other night so that Papa wouldn't be alone.

Early one morning, Dakota was surprised when Elmer met him at his drafting table only moments after Dakota had arrived after his forty mile commute. Elmer looked at him and said, "Come with me. Bring your time card." The kid thought for sure he was going to be fired, but once they were alone in the office Elmer explained, "Dakota, I know that your father is sick. I have your time card. I want you to go home and be with your family. Get some rest. Don't worry about your job; it'll be here for you. You'll be paid for every day until you return." That was the most amazing gesture Dakota had ever experienced. Teary-eyed, Dakota thanked him and went home. Dakota knew that even if Papa didn't need him, he needed to be with his papa.

Over the next few weeks Papa went downhill fast and needed to be taken to the hospital for care. Danny was with them the day when, to Dakota's surprise, Papa told Ellie in a very weak voice; "I want Jesus in my life before I die." Ellie got a pastor to come to the hospital where Papa invited Jesus into his life as he breathed his last breath. On Friday, October 13, 1961, Papa died.

The kid died a little that day also. It was so difficult to grasp and understand Papa was never coming home. Most of Kid Dakota's tears came that day because he was helpless to do anything to save his dad. The cancer killed his papa. This young man witnessed his 48-year-old papa go from a 180-pound strong guy to 90 pounds of skin and bone and it was devastating. Dakota had no regrets about standing at Papa's bedside night after night even when it was so damn emotionally painful. Dakota discovered how much he truly loved his papa. Papa's death was a major blow to the kid. Dakota never really got over the pain of seeing his papa die. The experience was just too awful. Papa was gone.

SEVEN

A New Look at Life

Dakota's beloved military aircraft

After Papa passed away, the broken-hearted kid returned to work a much more mature young man. The kid was growing up fast, even discovering a gal named Nancy at church. Dakota was attending Sunday services on a regular basis and he also joined the Sunday night young adults group. One gal caught his eye so he boldly walked up to her afterwards and asked if he could take her home. The relationship started slowly because Dakota had moved to be closer to his job and was only at his mom's on the weekends. Over time, Nancy and Dakota would go for ice cream after the young adults meeting.

Change was taking place at the aerospace company. They offered Dakota a transfer to another location much closer to his mom's home, with a much shorter drive. The transfer was also a major upgrade to a new position. Dakota would be assigned to work on the most amazing aircraft at that time, the A3J/A5 Vigilante. This military plane was the premier reconnaissance attack airplane of its time. The A3J flew at Mach 2.0 speed and was able to climb to a world record altitude of 91,450 feet. It was the largest, fastest attack plane to operate from a naval aircraft carrier, making it a strategic war plane from the sea.

Dakota glanced around his new surroundings at his new co-workers. The kid realized he was no longer doing kid's stuff. He was now working elbow-to-elbow alongside aerospace engineers and the top designers of the day. These were the book-smart people with brains. Dakota was learning much more "hands-on" than by reading books. Dakota never thought he would be working on any aircraft, especially not such a plane as the A3J. It was a rocket with wings, an amazing aircraft.

The many times Dakota sat quietly listening as a youngster, attempting to identify each aircraft by shape and sound had fostered a passion for planes. Many different types of war planes flew overhead because they were being built near where the kid lived. Papa encouraged his boy to learn about the aircraft. Papa brought home pictures of the aircraft for Dakota from the companies that built them.

Dakota learned fast—he enjoyed studying the aircraft specs and learning the names of each plane. He could read if he enjoyed the subject. Dakota showed his older brother he had some smarts, too.

His favorite plane in the 1940s was the P38, a fast, unconventional looking aircraft. Powered by two Allison V12 engines, the P38 had an all-aluminum skin and could fly 500 miles per hour. The 50 caliber machine guns on front of the pilot module made the P38 a very impressive looking war plane.

Dakota was no longer the kid who stood in amazement looking upward at the sounds of military aircraft. Now he was hands on, helping to build military aircraft like the A3J that the next generation of kids would look up in amazement to see. You could say he was living his dream.

Unfortunately, Dakota's life always traveled along two concurrent parallel tracks. His work life was amazing. He thoroughly enjoyed every aspect of his job duties; that was all good. But the pain from Papa's death was the opposite. Dakota was haunted by the images of his papa, all too young and much too soon lying in bed, dying, his skin sticking to the bed sheet and peeling off. On the weekends, when Dakota walked back into his family home, the memories of Papa caused tears every time: the front door where Papa walked in after work; the bedroom where Papa wasted away; the home to which Papa would never return. So many emotions and images to process.

Mom Ellie didn't want to stay in the house. It had too many memories for her just like it did for Dakota. She moved to a small, older home down the street, a nice little place. Before Papa's death, Mom had been working for a large department store chain in the accounting department at their massive headquarters in Los Angeles. Continuing to work helped to take her focus off the loss of the only man she ever loved. Losing Papa changed her, and not for the better.

Dakota moved from Orange County back to the neighborhood of his first apartment, the one where he drank beer with his neighbor, Charlie, the Hawaiian guy. Dakota's attempts to brush away the images of Papa's last days were futile; the memories of his papa brought tears. In response to the pain and the hurt, Dakota drank and cross-dressed, almost every day. Enflamed by too much drinking, Dakota's struggle with his gender issues became worse. During this time, Dakota purchased a fast motorcycle, a 1969 Triumph 650 Bonneville, for some road riding therapy to clear his head.

After many months, the A3J project wrapped up and Dakota was moved to an even more prestigious project: the Apollo space missions. President Kennedy's space race was on and Dakota was there in the middle of it, on a team of very talented guys. Dakota was about to learn a new word: cryogenics, the study of the behavior of materials at very low temperatures, under minus 238 degrees Fahrenheit.

The team's charge was to develop specifications for electric connectors so that they could function in the extreme cold of outer space. Not many scientists of the time knew much about the effects of extremely low temperatures on materials. Some metals fell apart, or even exploded. This small team took the specifications handed down by NASA and developed connectors for the guidance systems and ignition systems for all the Apollo missions.

Dakota was dating this great gal, Nancy, on a regular basis. He had been taking her to movies and to the ice cream shops for some time. One night Dakota and Nancy were on their way to a young adult event at church. Their friends were seated in the front; they were sitting together in the back.

Dakota was so smitten with her that, in a playful way, with no fanfare at all, the Kid amazed himself and her. Dakota proposed. This not-so-classy kid just turned toward Nancy, looked her in the eyes, and blurted, "Nancy, I think we should get married."

Nancy, with a hint of sarcasm, knowing him to be a big kidder, brushed him off, "Do you really? Yeah, sure you do."

Dakota, trying to sell her on the idea, replied, "No, really. I'm not kidding. I think we should get married."

Nancy, "Dakota, you're kidding me, right?"

Dakota, "No, really, I think we should get married."

Almost as shocking as Dakota's impromptu proposal was Nancy's quick response. She looked at Dakota, smiled and said, "Okay, let's get married!"

"Nancy and I are going to get married. We're really going to get married!" whooped a shocked Dakota to the friends in the front.

Their friends laughed. Dakota was always being funny. Like Nancy, they first thought that he was joking around, as usual.

This marriage idea became real, even though Dakota was struggling with deep-rooted gender issues. Dakota knew he needed to tell Nancy about his gender issues prior to their upcoming marriage, but that would come in due time. Before any real plans could be made, Dakota knew he needed to ask Nancy's father for permission to marry his only daughter.

Paternal approval wasn't assured; in fact, it was in great doubt. Nancy's father was a hard-core, serious, upper-income guy and he made it known he wasn't fond of Dakota, his motorcycle, or his drinking.

Nancy set a time on a Saturday morning when she knew her dad was going to be home for Dakota to come over and approach him with the proposal of marriage. So on that Saturday Dakota came riding up, motorcycle roaring, into the driveway. It was difficult to know who was more arrogant or confrontational—Dakota or Nancy's dad. Dakota knew the sound of the motorcycle alone would send chills down Nancy's dad's back. The two were about to face off, like two cowboys in an old western gun fight.

Dakota, with an arrogant swagger, walked toward Nancy's back door. Before he could finish walking up the driveway, the back door opened. Standing in the doorway was Nancy's dad. Loudly, in a gruff tone, he barked at Dakota, "Park that damn bike on the street. I don't want it in my driveway."

Dakota was put a bit off balance, but he politely responded, "Okay."

Under the watchful eyes of Nancy's very grumpy dad, Dakota walked back to his motorcycle, grabbed the handle bars and, without firing up the engine, rolled it into the street. For the second time Dakota walked toward the back door, knowing from her dad's tone and body language that a confrontation was brewing. Both were prepared to stand their ground, toe-to-toe if necessary. It would be necessary.

Dakota could see polite small talk was out of the question. He knew if he asked for Nancy's hand in marriage, her dad would say no. Quickly he decided to rephrase the exchange to something that didn't need a yes or no answer.

"Nancy and I are going to get married this June in Las Vegas. We wanted you to know you're invited to the wedding."

With that opening shot, World War III began. The gloves were off, if they were ever on.

"The hell you are! I'll make sure that you don't get married to my daughter."

Dakota fired back with both barrels. "We're getting married, whether you like it or not."

Nancy's father exploded and shouted, "Get the hell out of here now. This conversation is over."

Dakota gladly turned tail as fast as he could, like his butt was on fire, his adrenaline racing. His legs couldn't propel him to his motorcycle fast enough. The exchange put some fear in him. He swiftly straddled the bike and roared away without another word, thinking to himself, "That went well, don't you think?" It looked hopeless. But what Dakota didn't know was he had an ally: Nancy's mom, who would step into the fray on her daughter's behalf. She always liked Dakota for his humor and upbeat attitude. In contrast, Nancy's dad didn't have one ounce of humor in his entire body. He was book smart, no doubt about that. He was a rich guy who saw Dakota as an uneducated troublemaker.

Nancy lived at home with her parents and she was well acquainted with the family dynamics. As much as her dad was a terror towards Dakota, Nancy knew her mom was stronger than her dad. Her mom let Nancy know one thing for sure, "Nancy, your dad will agree to the wedding. Don't worry one bit about that; I'll handle your father."

Later on that same day Nancy was able to call Dakota and give him an update. After Dakota had left, her dad approached Nancy and made her an offer: she would get a new Pontiac Firebird, if she agreed not to marry Dakota. When Nancy's mom found out, she exploded. She wouldn't stand for her husband's bribery of a new car. Nancy's mom let the old geezer know who the real boss was.

Not long after Nancy's call, Dakota got a call from Nancy's dad. "I see you two are determined to get married, BUT the wedding will not be in Las Vegas. Her mother and I will plan the wedding and we'll pay for everything."

This change of heart in Nancy's dad came after he ran smack dab into an angry wife who was furious that he was trying to prevent her only daughter's marriage to the young man she loved. Nancy's mom liked Dakota. But the chill on the relationship between Dakota and Nancy's dad never thawed; it was always tough going. Dakota wasn't a bad guy, just immature, especially in dealing with conflict.

So with everyone's approval Dakota and Nancy moved forward with wedding plans. They made an appointment with the pastor at the small church they were attending, the same church where Dakota and his brother Danny had been baptized many years earlier.

Nancy knew about Dakota's long running battle with gender issues and she didn't think it was a big thing. But how should they go about telling the pastor who would marry them? The answer came from Nancy: "Let's not talk about it on our first visit. We can bring it up later if we want to."

But after the first meeting Nancy started thinking she wanted Dakota to explain everything to the pastor so he could help Dakota. Dakota called the pastor to make the second appointment.

The pastor asked Dakota, "Why do you want to talk with me?"

Dakota thought he may as well let him know up front: "Well, I've struggled for years with dressing in girl's clothes and sometimes with thinking I'm a female inside a male body."

If the pastor was shocked, his calm reply didn't show it, "Well, that must be very difficult for you to hide. I do think you should come in so we can talk."

The appointment was set for 8:30 p.m. At the appointed time, Dakota opened the tall door which led to the church offices. He walked all the way from the front door down the hallway to the pastor's office in the back; the hollow sounds of his footsteps on the floor filling every inch of space. He arrived at the pastor's office, feeling awkward, knowing the subject tonight would be his struggle with gender issues. He pushed gently on the slightly opened door. Dakota didn't know how the pastor would react. He had sounded okay on the phone, but meeting in person, face-to-face, might bring the unexpected. Dakota had no idea how unprepared he was for what happened next.

The room was dark; only one small light cast a glow at the back of the office. Dakota could barely see the pastor in the shadows.

The pastor's voice came to him very quietly, "Come in. Sit down. We can talk now."

What caught Dakota's eye were the items sitting on the edge of the desk: a bottle of a whiskey alongside a six pack of beer.

The pastor didn't get up from his desk, but staying seated, said to Dakota, "Have a beer or some Jack Daniels. I brought it for us so we could talk and relax tonight."

Now this was kind of freaky and unsettling, strange and uncomfortable. Dakota quickly said, "No, thanks."

The pastor asked, "Tell me all about your cross-dressing."

That felt a little more normal. Dakota started explaining why he was there.

"It started as a game of dress-up at my nana's house. I was only about four years old. Ever since then, I haven't been able to stop or avoid the feelings."

The pastor asked, "Why do you want to talk about this now?"

Dakota, "Nancy wanted me to tell you, to see if you could help me stop."

The pastor took a sip of whiskey, then opened a beer and starting drinking it. Dakota sat silently, not speaking; he didn't feel safe or comfortable watching the pastor drink alone. Dakota wasn't so sure now he wanted to talk about his issues. Dakota fell into a long period of silence but then the pastor started asking more questions. Dakota reluctantly talked about his cross-gender obsession, an obsession that wouldn't go away. By this time the pastor had consumed a good portion of the adult beverages. Empty beer cans stood where full ones had been, and the whiskey bottle was no longer full. The counseling session was about to take another unexpected turn.

The pastor abruptly stood up in the dimly lit room. Dakota's eyes had adjusted so he could see the clergyman was wearing his full length black robe, the kind worn for Sunday service. The pastor took a single step forward to stand right in front of Dakota and placed his hand at the top of the black robe. Dakota could see the pastor had his hand on the zipper that ran the length of the robe. No one was talking; the air was still. The pastor slowly began unzipping his robe until it fell fully opened. He was naked underneath. He sat down and then he sprawled out naked on the floor. Dakota was in total shock.

His naked pastor was looking up, beckoning him to come to him, saying, "Dakota, come here to me. Come here, please. This will be our little secret."

Dakota wanted no part of any more secrets; he had had enough of that sick stuff. The pastor had misjudged Dakota thinking the cross-dressing was a sign Dakota was a homosexual. Tears flew to Dakota's eyes. Dakota was mad and wanted this pastor to know.

"I'm not like that. Not at all."

With the naked pastor still on the floor, Dakota made a quick exit from the office.

Dakota couldn't wait to tell Nancy what had happened. She was astounded—the pastor was married and had two kids. It didn't take long for Dakota and Nancy to select another church and another pastor for their wedding. No more discussing Dakota's gender issues with anyone. It seemed clear that everyone, like the pastor had, would think Dakota was homosexual when he wasn't.

Rightly or wrongly, this experience caused Dakota to conclude that people would always misunderstand. Sharing the issue wasn't safe; getting help was out of the question. What happened in the pastor's office was one more layer added on top the many other layers of issues, all kept tamped down by frequently drinking to excess.

In spite of the raging internal conflict inside, Dakota remained rock-solid focused and very dependable at work. Dakota was a good listener and he applied this skill to learning from the brilliant people who surrounded him. He excelled at "hands on" learning. Dakota could hardly take it in that he had a job in the aerospace industry, let alone that he was working on the Apollo program. The NASA Apollo program was the future of space exploration and Dakota was in on the ground floor.

The greatest minds in the world were applying their talents to the quest to explore outer space and here was a kid with major gender issues right in the midst of it. While seated at his drafting table, Dakota could see the famous scientist Wernher Von Braun seated in his office only fifteen or twenty feet away. Von Braun was known as "the father of rocket science" and he was the chief architect of the Saturn V rocket used to send people to the moon.

In November of 1963 tragedy struck the country. President Kennedy was dead, shot by an assassin while riding in an open car in Dallas. Dakota was sitting at his drafting table when the news came. The blow to the nation was almost impossible to comprehend. Yet the country showed its strength that day by moving forward without John F. Kennedy as leader of the nation.

One year later, Dakota became a father. Much to the delight of both he and Nancy, their family expanded to include a baby daughter. But Dakota also knew fatherhood came with great responsibility.

Over the next few years Dakota worked steady on the Apollo program team. But even with the very best engineers in the world, no one could have seen what was coming because even the best cannot always be perfect. On January 27, 1967, three astronauts died in a fire inside the Apollo command module on the launch pad during a preflight test. NASA halted all work on the Apollo program until a full investigation could uncover the reasons for the fire.

Day after day, Dakota sat at his desk, doing nothing. Unless the investigation came to a conclusion soon, furloughs would be next. It didn't take a rocket scientist to figure that out. Sitting idle and waiting for the results of some government review was pure torture. Kid Dakota needed to keep busy. Besides, Nancy was pregnant with their second child and the responsibility of providing for his family weighed heavily on Dakota. He went looking for a new career.

Dakota always noticed cars, and he noticed that his neighbor across the street came home in a new car almost every night. Dakota wasn't bashful, either. He grabbed a couple of beers from the refrigerator and went across the street to introduce himself.

With a beer extended and a big smile, Dakota gave a greeting, "Hello there! My name is Dakota. I live over there in the gray house."

"Hi. My name is Ed and thanks for the beer."

"I see you in a different new car almost every night. Where do you get a job like that?"

Ed explained, "I work for a car company. It's funny you ask because they're looking to hire someone to do warranty auditing at dealerships."

The two talked and sipped beer late into the night. Ed agreed to get Dakota an employment application and help get it going.

After Ed brought him the application, Dakota wasted no time. He filled it out and handed it back that same week. Dakota wanted the job for sure. The prospect of working around cars was terribly exciting.

"Don't expect anything too quick," Ed told Dakota. "They don't move too fast in reviewing applications. But don't worry; they'll call you in for an interview."

Dakota knew where he wanted to work, but waiting? He was already playing the waiting game in his current job. Sitting all day with nothing to do and the anxiety of not knowing each day when he walked in if this was the day he would lose his job were driving him crazy. No more waiting for him. Dakota took a job at a nearby department store. At least that had purpose and activity.

Finally, about three months later, Dakota got the call. The car company wanted to interview him for the position. Dakota drove to the address near the Los Angeles airport and aced the interview with his capable, friendly and humorous style of communicating. He was offered the job on the spot. Without any hesitation, Dakota accepted. Two weeks later he parted ways with the old time department store and started his new career in the automobile business.

Shortly thereafter, Dakota became a father for the second time, this time a baby boy. "Nice," he thought, "A boy and a girl." This papa was going to make sure his boy would understand he was a boy and a damn good one, for sure.

Dakota's gender issues persisted in tandem with the ever increasing consumption of alcohol. By the time he was thirty-two, the years of frequent drinking had caused some real damage. He was vomiting up blood every day and suffered from extreme abdominal pain, consequences of too much drinking in the dozen years since his father died. He really needed his papa, back then and even now.

Dakota had been warned by his doctor to ease up on the drinking because it was causing damage. One evening at home Dakota felt excruciating pain in his abdomen. He turned toward Nancy, hunched over and said, "I'm really sick."

Alarmed, she said, "What's wrong?" as she watched Dakota dash toward the bathroom. She followed him and arrived in time to see he was throwing up blood.

Noticeably scared, she spoke in an elevated tone, "Dakota, I've got to take you to the hospital."

Defiantly, Dakota replied, "No!" as he got off his knees on the bathroom floor and went to lie down on the bed. Dakota thought he was going to die; he hurt so much.

His wife had seen enough. "You're going to the hospital now; get in the car," she demanded.

Dakota reluctantly accepted the invitation for that ride he didn't want. He was going to the hospital emergency room.

It didn't take long for the medical doctors to determine surgery had become absolutely necessary. Dakota's stomach was bleeding internally from a hiatal hernia caused by alcohol abuse. His stomach was being sucked up into his esophagus. Repairing the damage would require extensive surgery to the esophagus and part of his stomach;

The recovery was stressful. It was difficult to walk, eat and sleep without pain. The doctor prescribed large amounts of Valium to reduce Dakota's anxiety. Valium was a pain medication known to be addicting, just as addicting as alcohol. The surgery and medication did nothing but send Dakota into increased desires to change genders.

For nearly a year after the stomach surgery Dakota suffered from frequent esophageal spasms that caused him to faint at work. All the while, in Dakota style, he rarely complained and never let on that he was suffering. He wouldn't allow anything get in the way of working because work somehow helped push away the girl that was in his head.

For the next four or five years, Dakota's life continued on the same track. He was always trying to escape the damn dress in his head and the desire to change genders. It was crazy, he thought, to have this obsession he couldn't stop. This married man, father of two, was coping with his internal struggles in the only way he knew how: lubricated with alcohol and cross-dressing in secret.

In spite of his physical and emotional obstacles, Dakota was very successful in his new career. He loved what he was doing, and especially he loved the people at the auto company. Dakota's heavy drinking didn't hold him back, rather the opposite. He fit right in. In the automotive industry, relationships which led to advancement and promotion were formed over drinks at lunch and in bars after work. As his career improved, his drinking got worse. Everything appeared great on the outside, but, in fact, things were much worse than ever on the inside.

EIGHT
No Place to Turn

The Ph.D.'s Union St. office

Dakota, after battling all his life against his desire to dress and live as a female, could see no end in sight to the conflict. He confided in his best friend and his best friend's wife about the struggle he was having, about thinking he would be happier as a woman. Their hearts went out to him. They suggested that Dakota talk with a nurse they knew and trusted. Maybe she had some insight into how to get him some help. The nurse suggested he find a doctor that specialized in administering hormones. Dakota looked at the various ads in the Los Angeles Yellow Pages and selected one.

But Dakota kept his plans from his wife, Nancy. It was too shameful to admit it to this woman whom he had known since he was a teenager and who was the mother of his two children, that he wanted to experiment, dabble, you might say, in the world of cross-gender behavior.

His drinking was as extreme as ever. The episode of vomiting blood and subsequent stomach surgery hadn't diverted him at all. He didn't hide his drinking. Everybody was drinking in those days. Drinks at lunch and having a few with buddies after work were part of the automotive culture. Everything centered around drinking.

Dakota found it was as easy to get prescriptions from certain medical practitioners for hormones as it was to purchase a loaf of bread from the store. The doctor Dakota saw wanted him to have the hormones. Just show the doctor the money; nothing else mattered or was required. With no other place to turn, Dakota took the transgender off ramp and began taking female hormones. This road wasn't heavily traveled and would lead Dakota into the unknown.

One day Dakota called the doctor's office for another appointment and the gal on the other end of the line said that she would need to refer him to another doctor for further treatment—his doctor was no longer practicing medicine. Later, in the newspaper, Dakota found out why. The doctor had been arrested for practicing medicine without a license. The referral doctor was a legitimate M.D. and continued writing prescriptions for Dakota for hormones. Dakota began to believe that the hormones would fix his gender issues. Otherwise, why did the doctors prescribe them for him?

The hormone doctor was part of an underground cross-gender medical world. He helped Dakota find surgeons who performed various surgeries for feminizing the appearance of the gender troubled. You name it; they did it.

Talk about secrets. Dakota was keeping the hormones secret from Nancy, and now he was considering surgery without telling her anything about it. Dakota learned how to keep secrets. If this surgery was performed, it would be a secret from his wife; that was crazy.

Dakota's first feminizing surgical procedure was done in a doctor's office in Beverly Hills, the posh area of L.A. where Hollywood stars went for private medical care. Dakota needed to hide out during his recovery from surgery so he stayed with his best friends because their nurse friend could come over every day and check on his recovery. In another unfortunate twist in Dakota's life, the sutures broke and a gaping hole opened in his abdomen. The Beverly Hills surgeon, according to the nurse friend, had botched the procedure and a major infection set in. It was so bad the nurse took Dakota by the hand and drove him to the closest emergency room. But when hospital determined it was due to a botched surgical procedure, they refused to give him any treatment at all. Dakota was now in a world of hurt in more ways than one. First, the infection was life-threatening if not stopped quickly. Second, he would have to tell his wife everything.

Dakota telephoned his wife from his friend's house.

"Hello, Nancy. I need to tell you I'm so, so sorry. I really messed up big this time."

Nancy had had many conversations with Dakota like this before. Times when he promised to be home after work and called, clearly drunk, to say he couldn't. Times when he wrecked the car. Times when he didn't call, but snuck into the house much later than he was expected, long after everyone else in the family was in bed. He was on a business trip; what was it going to be this time?

Dakota could hear in her voice great disappointment.

"Just tell me; are you all right?"

The emotional pain of his deception cut him to his core.

"I'm not okay. This was all my fault. I have a big hole in my abdomen that's infected."

Nancy responded, "Do you need me there with you?"

"No, I just want you to know how awful I feel about this. I'll keep in touch but I don't want you to see me messed up like this."

This botched cosmetic surgery was a horrible turn for Dakota in resolving his gender issues and a big blow to his marriage. Dakota was sick inside his head and sick from the surgical infection. The nurse would help him as would his friends. His first gender-related surgery nearly caused his death and left a mess of massive scar tissue on his abdomen and emotional scars for Nancy. Dakota felt so utterly foolish, but felt he really had no choice.

Within two weeks Dakota was recovered enough to go home to make amends with his wife and try to regain her lost trust. She had every right to give up on him. They loved each other, but coping with Dakota's drinking and gender struggles was taking a toll on Nancy.

The doctors said changing genders would help his gender issues, but this first surgery only made things worse. His internal schizophrenic voices continued telling him he was a female inside and a male body outside. Dakota grasped at treatments, but nothing was helping.

The drinking, the gender issues and now the addition of hormone pills and estrogen injections only made Dakota more unstable and confused. Anytime he was away on a business trip, he secretly dressed in female clothing in his hotel room. When he was traveling out of town, he fell deeper in into the gender abyss. Alcohol helped numb the unhealthy psyche. Everything he was doing was only making things worse.

Dakota needed to be around his family to help rein in his behaviors. Being with his family anchored him psychologically. Dakota truly loved being a father and a husband. He was able to set aside his gender issues by enjoying the family. He had his good moments—taking the family out to nice restaurants, enjoying weekend events at Lake Tahoe, staying in the coastal cities of California and in the mountains—all things they all enjoyed. Many times the family took their vacation at a mountain conference center that focused on the biblical foundations of family.

Dakota loved his kids and enjoyed the identity they gave him of father. He treated his daughter to special father-daughter dinner dates at fancy restaurants of her choosing. With his son, Dakota took weekend trips away to father-son retreats attended by a hundred or so other dads and sons. Dad called his son "little buddy" because they were good buddies; that was sure. Dakota never lost the love he had for his kids.

Dakota was in love with being dad and a husband but oh, he had problems. No road map existed for the road Dakota was traveling, no GPS; just a bunch of doctors intent on steering him toward a gender change with unknown consequences. If Dakota made a wrong turn on this road, there was no turning around—the way back was far too rough.

Back at work, Dakota totally amazed himself when he took first place nationally in a sales contest competing against forty-two other reps from around the country. He had thrown himself into the contest, giving it his best. Even so, he was amazed when he won. As a direct result, soon after, he was promoted. In 1981, just past his fortieth birthday, Dakota was appointed national port operations manager reporting directly to the corporate vice president for a major Japanese automobile manufacturer.

This upper management position allowed Dakota great freedom to travel to all ports of entry for automobile cargo in the United States. During his many travels to the port city of Oakland, California, he gradually became aware of a man in the nearby city of San Francisco who was reported to be the best in the United States in dealing successfully with gender issues. The doctor was only too happy to schedule an appointment to talk with Dakota. All his life Dakota yearned to be evaluated and get some help and now it seemed within his grasp. This Ph.D. doctor was a nationally known professional who had been treating people with gender issues for many years. Dakota was eager and excited; he was going to be evaluated by the best. He specifically wanted to know if surgery, male to female, would end the thirty-seven years of gender issues he had endured.

For Dakota this would be a special appointment. He booked a hotel room near the doctor's office so he could dress as a female for the appointment in order to show the evidence of his struggle. Dakota wanted to dress to impress. He prepped in an outfit he purchased especially for the occasion—blonde wig, skirt, blouse and heels. Looking like any female office worker in the city, he walked the short distance to the Ph.D.'s Union Street office.

Dakota arrived at his destination and opened the office door. Before him stood a tall, slender man who didn't look to be yet forty years old.

"Hi, Doctor!"

The man responded, "You must be Nicole."

The doctor was correct. Nicole was Dakota's female name; at least it was in 1981.

Dakota started by asking the big questions, the ones for which he desperately wanted answers.

"Do I need the surgery? Will it provide the treatment I have always needed?"

The doctor told Nicole/Dakota, "The surgery is highly successful, but let's not get ahead of ourselves. I have some questions that need answers about how your desires to transition to female evolved."

Nicole/Dakota began to explain, saying, "It started around when I was little, around the age of four. From that point on, I felt like a girl was trapped inside me. Now I'm forty years old and still struggling."

In a flash, without asking any questions like he had originally said he would, the gender specialist delivered his diagnosis.

"You fit the profile of a transgender and most likely have been suffering from gender dysphoria all your life."

Dakota listened intently as the doctor went on to explain the diagnosis.

"I'm a real transgender? Really? Are you sure about this?" Dakota asked.

"Yes, you are. I would like to see you again next week, if that's possible."

Nicole/Dakota was euphoric at the idea that his gender troubles would come to an end, but disappointed surgery would be necessary for treatment. Surgery seemed a little crazy to him. But no one else had any better ideas for helping him. Dakota was desperate for treatment, anything that would bring him relief, and everywhere he turned, the options seemed limited. The troubled kid, now an adult, husband of over fifteen years and father of two kids, was exhausted from the lifelong battle.

Surgically changing genders was the only known treatment being offered for his gender dysphoria.

Dakota had questions, lots of questions, but few real answers. A week later, Nicole/Dakota went back to the Union Street office as doctor had requested. This time, the doctor took time to describe his credentials to Dakota.

"Several of us in the gender field have come together to form an organization that focuses on gender issues. It's named for Harry Benjamin—you might have heard of him? He pioneered the field. I'm the chairman of the committee to develop the 'standards of care,' that is, proper treatment protocol for people like you who feel they were born as the wrong gender. We wanted to ensure that patients with gender dysphoria are properly evaluated, diagnosed and treated. The standards of care were published recently and I'm actually the primary author of them."

"I'll write an approval letter for your surgery so you can resolve your dysphoria and get on with your life."

Nicole was surprised approval came so readily, on the second appointment,

"Really? You're telling me changing genders is the answer?"

The Ph.D. doctor assured him, "You have all the known markers that tell me you'll benefit. Your struggle will be over after surgery."

Inside Nicole's head, thoughts were bouncing everywhere, like a pinball machine. Panic. Anxiety. Conflicting feelings of pain, fear and hope. Nicole/Dakota's mind raced to imagine some of the consequences of changing genders. He faced endings and endings are painful. One life, his life as Dakota, would end. Dakota would no longer exist. His marriage would end. Hope. The procedure held out a golden ray of hope; hope that the gender change and life as Nicole would be better than living with the struggle as Dakota. Fear. Nicole/Dakota had some fear that the results wouldn't be as helpful as the doctor predicted. After all, the procedure was new and not yet proven.

Nicole went back to the hotel room to switch her appearance back to that of Dakota and returned home. Dakota went back to work without telling anyone, especially not his wife, that he had been approved for the gender change surgery. Dakota felt the Ph.D. was correct in his assessment but without real proof, he had concerns. In the early 1980s, anyone who entered the gender blender had limited options. The few experts in the field quoted a few case studies that spoke of surgery providing wonderful success.

Dakota had told his wife he was using hormones as part of his treatment for his gender issues. Using cross-gender hormones causes physical and emotional changes. Dakota was facing a wicked cocktail of serious issues, all colliding like a multicar wreck. His marriage was in deep trouble. His core identity, the very foundation of himself, who he was, had always been tremendously turbulent. Now in his forties, Dakota knew only that the struggle had deepened. Would his strength remain to fight and pull him through, or would he fall under the weight of it all?

In spite of all that was going on internally, Dakota had the ability to push aside his difficulties and move up the ladder of corporate success. He loved working.

Dakota's new duties as national port operations manager were gobbling up extensive amounts of his time, far beyond the typical forty to fifty hour work week. Dakota's work week started on Sunday night on an airplane. Every day from Sunday through Friday, he was on a different flight. Red-eye flights became his hotel rooms.

The week started with an overnight flight from California to Puerto Rico via Florida. Through the remainder of the week, Dakota hopscotched from one port of entry to another: Puerto Rico, three ports on the East coast, Houston, three on the West coast and Hawaii. Unending fatigue came with this grueling schedule.

As if the travel weren't enough, Dakota's job required him to pay attention as each ship discharge its cargo of 5,000 cars. He was the man in charge of all the cars imported into the United States for his company. Once the cars left the ship, or were "discharged," and Dakota signed off on them and the cars became his responsibility.

Between the ship and the yard, however, was a zone that belonged to the port operator and the union longshoremen. Dakota's company contracted with the port operators to take the cars off the ship, move them to the storage yard, put several gallons of gas in each, and later, load them on the trains or trucks for delivery to the dealerships.

The cost of docking and discharging a ship at a port was staggering—nearly $20,000 per hour, so quick unloading was critical. Each car was individually driven off the ship by longshoremen who liked to see how fast they could drive, like little kids. Dakota had to keep a sharp eye out so that they didn't sneak a car damaged by their antics past him. The union had to be held accountable for cars they damaged. Dakota was responsible for removing the vehicle identification number, or VIN, tag so that the car couldn't be sold as new, and for preparing a report so that his company could invoice the union for the entire cost of the car. All damaged vehicles were scrapped.

No downtime and traveling every day did nothing but escalate the difficulty Dakota had with gender issues. Love for family is wonderful, powerful, and most often full of joy, but not so much for someone with unresolved gender issues masked by alcohol use. Dakota discovered the love he had for his wife and kids was outdone by his psychological issues. Dakota couldn't grasp in which direction he should turn. His usual knowledge of right and wrong was no help in these uncharted waters. Just because it felt right didn't make it right. Dakota was at the end of his emotional rope.

Just when it seemed that he could endure no more, along came an unanticipated situation that dialed up the pressure even more.

Dakota's job duties required him to follow up on problems reported by car dealers regarding cars delivered from the ports. He started getting complaints from many of the New Jersey dealers about the new cars that arrived at their dealerships: they were out of gas. It was so bad, they said, they had to get behind the cars and push them off the truck. Dakota thought this was a curious complaint because the company paid the port operators to put three gallons of gasoline in each vehicle as part of their contract. Three gallons had always been plenty. Even more curious, only the New Jersey dealerships were reporting the issue.

Dakota headed to the New Jersey port to investigate the dealer claims. At the port, Dakota parked the rental car and walked directly to the storage yard responsible for gassing cars. Dakota was known at the port of entry, so they thought nothing of seeing him walk through the main office to the outside storage yard where thousands of cars were parked at any given time, ready for delivery. He walked directly to the part of the yard where the gas trucks were. It wasn't fancy. It looked like an old-time gas station.

Dakota spied one of the gas truck drivers he knew from previous trips and asked him pointblank, "I want to know if you're making sure three gallons of gas gets in every one of our cars." The driver looked at him a little defensively and said, "No, they told us to stop gassing the cars. They said the order came from your company headquarters." Dakota's attitude changed because he knew something was wrong. No one was authorized to change a contractual agreement, ever. Dakota nodded his head and said politely, "Thank you. I wasn't aware of that." The gas truck driver snapped back at Dakota sarcastically, "Well, you sure as hell should know. You're the man from headquarters, right?" Dakota just kept walking toward the main office without another word.

The only thing Dakota knew was that the contract paid the port contractor $5 for each car to get gas. Each month, 8,000 cars came through the New Jersey port. Dakota did the math: $5 times 8,000 cars was $40,000 a month. The port operator got this monthly check from the company like clockwork, just for gassing the cars. The only problem was: the cars weren't getting any gas in return for the money. The dealers had good reason to file a complaint.

Dakota was puzzled. Who at his company had authorized the change? He needed to find out. Dakota decided to start first in the accounting office. Maybe they had some answers. Dakota walked briskly across the storage yard toward the main office and entered through the back door. Inside the office was a familiar face, Gloria, the manager of accounting, with whom he had talked many times regarding financial contract requirements. He always kept a good relationship with Gloria. This question regarding gas was important.

Hovering over her desk, Dakota said his "hello" but quickly got down to business and asked, "Gloria, do you have invoice payments you can show me for how much you are paying for fuel each month?"

Gloria looked up at Dakota like she had been caught with her hand in the proverbial cookie jar. She turned her body slightly away from Dakota as she responded, "Yes. I recall we only purchased $643 of fuel last month and only about $280 so far this month."

Dakota looked at her, searching her face for clues. They both knew a payment of nearly $40,000 a month came from the car company for gas. She turned red and looked real shaken like she had said too much.

"I don't have any more time to help you right now. Can you come back tomorrow?"

Dakota replied, "Okay, let's plan on it first thing in the morning." Out the door he went.

Dakota climbed back into the driver's seat of his rental car for the thirty-minute drive to his hotel. Being a creature of habit, he always stayed at the same hotel. When Dakota arrived at the hotel and approached the front desk to check in, the clerk said, "We have three urgent messages for you." Dakota frowned. Having three urgent messages waiting for him by the time he reached his hotel was highly unusual. He quickly scanned the slips of paper to see who called. One was from his boss, Dean, and another was from a coworker, Stephen, a member of Dakota's much-needed support staff back in California. The last of the three messages came from Gloria, the accounting manager at the port storage yard, who thirty minutes ago had said she was too busy to talk to him.

Dakota checked in to the hotel and went up to his room to return the calls. What he didn't know was that his brief investigation into the gassing of cars had set off a firestorm between the port operator and his boss, Dean. He called his boss first. "Dean, I got an urgent message to call you. How can I help?" Dean answered, "Yes, I got a call from Gloria. She told me you were asking questions about gassing cars. Tell me: why were you asking questions about how much gas they purchased?"

Dakota replied, "Well, several of our dealers reported their cars were running out of gas. When they arrived at the dealership, they needed to be pushed. So I wanted to know if the port operator was gassing the cars."

Dean, who was a jerk most of the time to everyone, came back in a very unfriendly tone, "Look, we have a special agreement with this port operator on the gassing of cars. Drop your investigation now. I'll personally take care of this. Don't tell anyone about your investigation; no one."

Dakota felt like a kid getting scolded undeservedly.

"I can't drop this. There's $40,000 dollars a month unaccounted for here. I think our accounting office needs to know about this so they can follow up and withhold payments if necessary."

Dean, clearly elevated and getting angrier, said, "I'm telling you, Dakota. Don't talk to anyone about this. I'll take care of it. If you don't do what I tell you, I'll have no choice but to write up an action of insubordination and put it in your file. This could be cause for your immediate termination."

Dakota couldn't believe what he was hearing. He wasn't a lightweight in any confrontation and he came back in an equally elevated tone, "You know, Dean, it would take some big balls to terminate the guy who uncovered a huge financial irregularity. So you better reconsider your words carefully because I won't stay quiet just because you tell me to."

With that Dean exploded, "Dakota, get your ass back here. I want you in my office by 9 a.m. tomorrow and keep your mouth shut."

Dakota sarcastically responded, "I'll be there, no problem. In fact, I look forward to talking to you about this! How about we call in accounting to our meeting, too?"

Click. Both Dean and Dakota hung up.

Dakota took a deep breath in an attempt to cool off. His adrenalin was pumping. But breathing didn't affect his anger; it continued to elevate. Dakota was now real curious about why Gloria from the port operator's office called with an urgent message. Dakota dialed and Gloria answered.

"Hello, this is Gloria in the accounting office. How can I help you?"

"This is Dakota. What happened after I talked to you earlier today? Tell me what is going on here?"

"This has gotten way out of hand. I don't want to get myself in trouble. I'm scared."

"Gloria, you know withholding gas from the cars is fraud. So whose idea was it? And why?"

Gloria voice was halting, even trembling. She started to break down as she explained the details.

"Dakota, your boss and my boss cooked up this idea between them. I was told to keep quiet and comply. A lot of people will get in big trouble. We haven't been gassing your cars for some time. Dean gets $15,000 a month from us each and every month. The money is laundered through a furniture store owned by a friend of his. My boss keeps $25,000. He only spends money on gas if they run out as they come off the ship."

"Oh, crap! You've got to be kidding me. This is huge! No wonder Dean told me not to say a word about this to our accounting office."

Gloria asked Dakota, "What are you going to do?"

"Dean ordered me to go back to the California office."

"Be careful. I think Dean is connected to some bad people in New Jersey. I think he wants to keep you from exposing him."

"Thanks, Gloria. I'll do what I need to do."

Dakota had his answer. It was Dakota's knuckleheaded boss, Dean, who set this scam in motion. It explained why Dean was so angry on the phone. It explained why the driver in the storage yard had said, "Well, you sure as hell should know. You're the man from headquarters, right?" Something as simple as gassing cars had been turn into racketeering and fraud. Dakota was shaken by this unwanted turn of events.

Now Dakota became even more curious about the third message he held in his hand, the one marked urgent from a member of his support staff. The caller, Stephen, sat just outside Dean's office in the California office. One of Stephen's responsibilities was taking and processing calls from port operations staff and car dealers reporting damage to cars. Calls came in at all hours from all over the country. Obviously, the calls received after office hours were recorded. But the company also authorized the recording of calls that Stephen received and answered during office hours because the vehicle identification numbers were lengthy and capturing them with accuracy was difficult. It helped the efficiency of the claim process to have a recording to reference later of the details of damage and the exact vehicle identification number.

Dakota dialed Stephen's number.

After the second ring, Stephen answered, "This is Stephen."

"Stephen, you called me with an urgent message. What's up?"

Stephen quickly got to the point, "Yes, I did. I got concerned when I heard Dean talking to someone about you. Dean is real pissed off, Dakota. You made him mad. He told whomever he was talking to that you needed to be stopped from telling anyone about the gas issue in New Jersey. So, I thought you should know right away that he is trying to get back at you."

"Dean wants to terminate my employment, that's all. He's plowing off steam. I'm not concerned."

Stephen replied, "I'm very concerned. Calls from Dean's phone can be recorded with both sides of the conversation. I'll record his calls if you tell me to."

Dakota: "Stephen, hell's bells! You know that's totally illegal."

Stephen: "Yes, but I think whatever Dean is doing is even more illegal. If the recording proves nothing I'll erase it. All that's easy, but listening in could provide proof of what he's up to."

Dakota: "This is some heavy crap. We could get in deep trouble. But if you're willing to do it, I say go ahead and record all his calls. It could come in handy if there's something big there."

Dakota thanked Stephen and hung up. To make it back to California in time for the next day's meeting, he would have to take a red-eye. He checked out of his room, intent on catching the next flight back to California. Sleeping was impossible anyway. He was stunned by what looked like underworld mob stuff. It was just crazy. Dakota was unwilling to step into this pile of dog poop. He wanted more answers.

Dakota got back to Los Angeles early the next morning, picked up his car and drove to the office having had almost no sleep on the overnight flight. He parked the car in his reserved parking space near the front door. As he walked to the front door, Dakota could see Stephen looking down from the second story, watching him. Dakota became even more curious as Stephen intercepted him on the stairway and motioned to Dakota to follow him. Dakota and Stephen went into the small conference room nearest the front door.

Dakota looked at Stephen. This grown man was shaking all over and visibly upset. Stephen grabbed Dakota's arm.

"I'm so glad you asked me to record the conversations. I have it on tape. Damn it, Dakota, you won't believe this. Dean contacted someone in New Jersey more than once. Dean is trying to locate someone who is willing to kill you."

Dakota wasn't buying it.

"Please tell me you're kidding me. This is a joke, right? What is this, some April fool's joke? Come on, Stephen, this has to be a joke. Dean isn't that stupid or that concerned."

"No joke. The call between Dean and this guy came in after hours. Dean must have stayed late so no one would be around to hear him."

Stunned, Dakota nodded his head in disbelief and said, "Wow! Thanks."

Dakota mind was running in circles around the thought, "This can't be happening. It's like a bad movie." He couldn't catch his breath. He felt like he had been kicked in the stomach. Dakota walked out of the conference room alongside Stephen and up to the stairs to the second level. They both got a cup of coffee and each went back to his desk.

Dakota was shaking so badly he couldn't hold his coffee cup steady in his hand. He kept thinking this was more like a movie script than real life. But unfortunately, at this point, Dakota's life was all too real. Whether or not he could take it in didn't stop it from unfolding. The morning meeting with Dean was approaching fast.

At 9 o'clock sharp, Dean approached Dakota's desk. In his hand, clearly visible, was a personnel file, probably Dakota's. To Dakota, he looked like a prison guard come to escort the condemned man to death row.

With no greeting, Dean said sternly, "Dakota, come with me to the executive conference room."

Trying to appear confident, Dakota quickly replied, "Sure, let's go."

Acting cool was going to take some effort. Dakota could feel his anxiety level skyrocket again just at the sight of Dean. He stood up but his legs stiffened and would hardly move. Trying to appear calm, Dakota brought along his still-full coffee cup but his hands were shaking so much he sat the cup on the edge of someone's desk as he walked by, without breaking his stride.

After the boss man selected one of the 25 chairs around the massive mahogany conference table, Dakota picked a chair facing him so he could keep eye contact. Opening the folder, Dean started talking.

"I have your personnel file here. Along with your file, I have your termination papers that you'll sign right now. You know why. Your insubordination cannot be tolerated."

Dakota felt his adrenalin pumping fast, but it was pumping him up for a fight. Dakota chose his words carefully and his scathing reply set his boss back in his comfortable seat.

"My little friend, you can take my termination papers and stick them up your ass. I'm not signing anything and I'm not going anywhere, but there is a chance you'll be going to jail."

Dakota could see the blood drain from Dean's face. His skin turned ashen as if he had seen a ghost. With that, Dakota pushed his chair back, stood and swiftly walked out of the massive conference room. Stephen later told Dakota that when Dean came back to his office his lily white face was broken out in big red blotches.

Now it was Dakota who was pissed off and he decided to talk with the executive vice president, Cliff, and tell him what was going on.

"Cliff, you need to know what's going on. Dean has scammed the company out of thousands of dollars in a money laundering scheme over gassing cars in New Jersey. Also the possibility exists that he ordered a contract hit on me to keep me quiet."

The EVP looked at Dakota as if he were an escapee from the third floor psyche unit. Cliff looked incredulous and in his typical quiet voice expressed some concern.

"You'd better be able to prove all this because I don't think it is possible."

Dakota picked up Cliff's phone and called Stephen.

"Come to the EVP's office immediately."

Then Dakota turned to Cliff and said, "I also thought this was impossible, but Stephen has some proof."

Right on cue, Stephen entered Cliff's office. Dakota looked at him and asked, "Do you have a recording of a call with Dean's voice where he is trying to order a contract hit on my life?"

Stephen answered, "Yes, I do."

Cliff turned to Dakota and asked, "How did you come to have this tape?"

Dakota explained, "At my request, Stephen taped all conversations Dean had yesterday. Dean was trying to terminate my employment today because yesterday I discovered he was getting $15,000 a month payments from port operations in New Jersey, laundered through a furniture store."

Cliff looked grim.

"Stay away from the office until I call you to come in. I'll get someone to fill your port duties temporarily. Just go home and let me get with our legal staff and with the human resources staff to document this so we can move forward with whatever is necessary."

Discovering fraud in the port operations, confronting his boss, learning of a hit on his life, and not knowing if he would be welcomed back to the company were extremely stressful on Dakota. But what made this the most stressful time of Dakota's life was something personal. His wife of sixteen years asked him to move out.

Our Kid Dakota was losing his desire to push through the pile of crap weighing him down. No windows for escape, no doors, all he could see was crap everywhere. At least, that's how he felt and he was too tired to fight. With the loss of the thing he valued most, his family, and with his career in jeopardy, he felt the cornerstone of his identity slipping away. He turned to drinking with a vengeance.

About two weeks later, Cliff called him and suggested it was a good time for Dakota start a new position at the company, one that didn't involve port operations. Cliff also told Dakota the rest of the story. His corrupt boss, Dean, agreed to resign from the company and the company agreed not to file any criminal charges. With the scheme fully exposed, everyone agreed the hiring of a hit on Dakota was now a moot point and Stephen's recording of the phone conversation would never be needed. The guy who owned the furniture store confessed to laundering money and admitted he had been giving Dean the money for the last few months. The port operator confessed and agreed to refund all the money that was stolen in the gassing contracts. All port contracts were changed to require proof that fuel was purchased for each car. The gassing loophole which had supplied Dean's slush fund was closed down for good.

Would a new position be enough to give Dakota a much-needed lifeline? Or, was Dakota's lifetime record of overcoming adversity coming to an end?

NINE

The Doctors' Treatment

The surgeon's Colorado office

Cliff did offer Dakota a great opportunity to remain with the company. Cliff liked Dakota. Obviously, due to recent events, he knew he could trust him. The automobile dealers had been craving a luxury division to compete against BMW. A small team was tasked with developing a completely new brand of high-end Japanese automobiles with separate name, branding and logo—not an easy task. Cliff created a new position, Assistant Manager of Product Development, reporting directly to him and under his wing, with responsibility for research and development for the new brand.

Prior to identifying the new brand name they referred to the new line simply as "second channel." The first step in product development was to identify the potential buyers through extensive demographic and income research studies.

Cliff made the case that Dakota should get this new assignment because of his highly successful career in the car industry and his prior background researching cryogenic materials for the Apollo space mission project. The company agreed. What the company didn't know was that their hand-picked candidate was a gender-twisted, alcohol-addicted man on the road to divorce.

For the first time in his automotive career Dakota had a position that wouldn't require him to travel. Unfortunately, it came too late—he had recently separated from his wife of sixteen years, due in part to the fact that he secretly had breast implant surgery, paid for by a dealer. At work, he wore an elastic compression strap to conceal his newly augmented chest. But he couldn't hide it from his wife and she was rightly angered by his self-indulgent actions.

What Dakota really wanted was to be a great father to the kids he loved. But he was powerless to untangle himself from his lifelong identity issues. He was incapable of showing his wife the love he felt, the love they both enjoyed in the early days of their marriage.

Being hand-picked to join a select team to create a totally new division of cars at a major automobile manufacturer was a big deal and everyone knew it. Rumors swirled that Dakota was in line to be corporate vice president over the division once it was launched.

Dakota career had been blessed starting with his early drafting days in the job with Elmer, then on to working on the amazing A3J military aircraft, followed by the Apollo moon mission project, and now on the next rung of success to executive level in the automobile industry. In each upward step, Dakota developed new skills and made an excellent income. Dakota worked steadily and hard in spite of his persistent gender issues.

Dakota's life was divided into three distinct parts. First, he was successful in his career. Second, he loved being a husband and a father; this was his greatest joy. Third, he was in constant turmoil over wanting to become a female on the outside to match what he felt was his true identity in his innermost being: female. It was a three-way tug of war and one way was already losing, the most important part: his family. Being the man he wanted to be seemed impossible to him. His psyche was fragile. The tug of war wore him out.

Dakota was racked with deep emotional conflict. He felt everything in his life hinged on being the best dad, husband and provider he could ever be. Without succeeding as dad and husband, how long could he hold on to the other good part of his life, his career? There Dakota was on top, but was he about to slip and fall?

From time to time, Dakota would pull the letter out, the one approving him for surgery, and re-read it. Having this letter in his possession meant that, at any time, Dakota could redeem it, along with thousands of dollars, in exchange for the radical genital reconstruction surgical change the Ph.D. had said would end his torment.

Dakota was living alone one block from the Pacific Ocean, free to cross-dress at home and go out alone at night in female clothes to walk along the strand. He was also easy walking distance to many of the best drinking bars at the beach. Many nights he sat drinking quietly ruminating in silent pain over one question, "What the hell happened to my life?" With no answers forthcoming, Dakota would sit and sip another drink.

Sitting alone in a bar surrounded by the noise set his mind off with wild ideas and thoughts. One lonely night sitting there he visualized a body of motionless water, smooth as glass. The water looked at rest, as if it were enjoying the afternoon sun that bounced off its surface. The water was quite at home, just soaking up the good life. Dakota thought, "If only I was that body of water undisturbed, peaceful without anything causing me ripples." But Dakota's life would never be smooth, pristine, peaceful or undisturbed; too much damage had been done.

The ripple effects always start small. Then they grow ever bigger and bigger until they are out of our control. The ripples can reach distances and head in directions that humans are powerless to grab, halt or change. Dakota just sat there with his drink, wishing nothing had ever happened to him as a young boy. Because the ripple effects of those early events just wouldn't stop.

At work, Dakota was enjoying his new position. He knew he had been given an amazing opportunity and he wanted to make the best of it. He loved his co-workers. Everyone was easy to work with and they had a fun time. But one thing became more important in Dakota's mind than his family, career or anything else—ending the raging conflict of genders. It just had to stop; he couldn't go on with it anymore. The final tug of war was being played out, and gender change was winning.

Dakota made arrangements with a surgeon in Colorado to have the procedure. The approval letter had been sent weeks earlier. Apparently no signs of unresolved psychological illness were at play in Dakota, at least not any that the medical professionals could see. Were there no bright neon signs flashing every day of his life?

Dakota was about to get the radical surgery and no one knew except the surgeon. There he was, carry-on bags in hand, boarding a Denver-bound plane, on a secret mission to change genders. No one knew: not his wife, none of his friends, not his employer. In Denver, he stepped onto a bus for long ride south to the small Colorado town known at the time as the "Gender Change Capital of the World."

As he arrived Dakota could see it wasn't much of a town at all. Just an old defunct mining town—no glitz, no glamor, with local town folk in their bib overalls looking out the coffee shop window to catch a glimpse of the latest surgically altered transgender. The sight of transgenders on the sidewalks, some prior to surgery, some after surgery, was commonplace, nothing to raise interest anymore.

From where the bus dropped him off, it was only a short walk to anywhere in town: his hotel, the surgeon's office, a café. Dakota checked into his hotel and changed into a red sweater top, tan skirt and red pumps, and went back out onto the streets of the small town. Now he was part of the transgender landscape, another man dressed as a woman, waiting for his surgery.

Dakota held in his hand a small slip of paper with the address of the surgeon's office. He was expected there for the pre-surgery appointment, a work-up for the gender surgery scheduled for the following day. He walked to the address and went directly up to the second floor for his appointment. Dakota was forty years of age.

Dakota would now use the female name Nicole on all surgical and hospital paperwork. Nicole checked in at the front desk and she was quickly ushered in to the surgeon's office.

The surgeon looked like George from the *Seinfeld* show: short, stocky, not inspiring confidence in Nicole even though she knew he had performed over 3,000 such surgeries.

The surgeon asked, "Are you ready for your big day tomorrow?"

Nicole answered, "Yes I'm ready. I need to end this lifelong conflict now, so I'm ready, that's for sure."

The Ph.D. approval letter verified that Nicole was a good candidate for this special surgery. The letter was the key that unlocked the door to both the appointment and the surgery. Only one more thing was needed. Nicole pulled out a wad of greenbacks from her red handbag. She handed the cash directly to the surgeon. The surgeon walked from the room and returned with a receipt.

Nicole thought the surgeon's office was rather strange-looking, like something from a Frankenstein horror movie. The old asphalt tile floor was dirty; the walls needed paint. The office looked as tired as Nicole felt. A few white well-used porcelain pans and tables scattered about the various rooms fostered an association in Nicole's mind. It looked like the movie set from the mental hospital in *One Flew over the Cuckoo's Nest*, a ghoulish place where instead of electric shock treatments, genitalia were targeted to be surgically altered, fashioned into something they were not, in order to treat the patient.

What was difficult to resolve in Nicole's mind was: was she suffering from a mental illness and had she arrived at the asylum? Or was she truly in a medical facility for a necessary surgical procedure? She knew there was no alternative treatment; all the doctors had told her surgery was the only treatment for gender dysphoria. Nicole's damn obsession to dress like a woman and to live like a woman meant that she should be a woman.

Nicole left the surgeon's office and walked the few blocks to the hospital for the pre-surgery blood tests. Once inside, she walked down the hall toward the office labeled "Surgical Intake." Nicole slowly opened the door and entered, and introduced herself to the woman behind the counter.

"My name is Nicole. I'm here for surgery tomorrow. What do I need to do?"

The woman replied, "Well, there are some fees to pay and papers to sign authorizing the surgery here at the hospital."

In the next split second, Nicole felt the enormity, the radicalness, in fact, the craziness, of continuing with the proposed surgery. She was in full panic. Without another word, Nicole turned toward the same door where moments before she had entered. She moved as if the building was on fire and she needed to escape with her life. As fast as her red pumps would take her, she exited the hospital. Once outside, Nicole continued her brisk pace back toward the surgeon's office. As she walked she muttered to herself, "What is happening to me? How did I get to this point? What am I doing!?"

Good questions, but she had no answers at all, just more questions. She wasn't having surgery the following day; that was certain. Nicole arrived at the surgeon's office. She didn't wait long to talk to him.

"I just cannot go through with the surgery. Can I get any kind of refund?"

The surgeon was polite and said, "Yes, we can give you fifty percent of your money back."

Nicole thought that her walk to the hospital and back was an expensive few blocks, but said, "Thank you. I'll take the fifty percent and go home."

The surgeon acted as though he had seen this reaction before and said, "You can come back any time. We'll keep your approval letter on file." He handed Nicole the refund money and left her there alone.

The cash in her hand, tears began to well up in her eyes. Mascara was running. She was broken, full of unbearable pain. Pain in her gut, pain in her heart. Pain from years of struggling to overcome these desires. Pain from holding the secrets from the wife, kids, friends, everybody, was becoming more than she could bear. Shame from hiding her thoughts and feelings, from hiding the cross-dressing and the feminizing procedures. It was as if there were two people sharing the same body. But neither Nicole nor Dakota knew what to do to be whole.

But on that day, at that time, Nicole knew that surgery wasn't the answer, at least not now. She didn't want to be Nicole. She wanted to be Dakota. She was determined to try being Dakota again. She waited at the bus stop, to start the long journey home.

Back at the beach apartment, Nicole changed to Dakota again. At least he could look like a husband and father even if he was just twisted remnant of his old self. But the experience of the aborted trip made Dakota deeply depressed, exhausted and even more confused. All the gender issues had become too complicated. It was like a rat's nest of wires in his head, all tangled in a knot he couldn't pull apart.

In total desperation, Dakota wanted to talk to his wife and he called her from his apartment.

"Nancy, it's me. I'm so sorry to call you like this. I know I have caused you so much pain already. But do you think you could give me just one more chance?"

Nancy wasn't happy to hear the request, but she was worried about him and showed her compassion.

"You don't sound good at all. You can come for the night tomorrow and stay in the guest room."

After all these years she still wasn't turning her back on him.

Dakota blubbered on, "I'm so sorry this gender stuff has built a wall between us. I just don't know what to do and I can't make it go away."

Nancy, understanding, said, "Yes, I know. You have fought hard for as long as I have known you." Then turning sorrowful she said, "Dakota, this has gone on much too long. It's scaring me. I just don't know how to help you. In fact, I know I can't help you."

Dakota, broken, said, "We can talk more when I get there tomorrow night, if that's okay."

Nancy said, "Yes, I'd like that."

Dakota went to the office the next day and worked his normal day, acting as if the events of the past few days hadn't happened. After work he drove the one hour back to the home where his wife and kids lived.

Nancy opened the door and gave Dakota a little hug, no smile, then walked him to the guest room. He placed his things on the bed and went to see the kids who were in the back yard. As he observed his kids playing, he became overwhelmed with guilt, shame and sorrow. He knew they had never signed up for a dad who was selfish and placed his gender issues ahead of his own kids. The kids deserved much more than this mess.

Later that night after the kids were in bed, Nancy and Dakota sat and talked. Dakota was trying to ease himself of the burden of the secret trip to Colorado that almost took his genitals. He wanted to open up and talk to Nancy about what he had done. Dakota felt like he had ice cubes in his gut as he struggled with how to tell her. Nancy could feel the chill between them. When Dakota looked down at the floor instead of in her eyes, she knew that whatever he came to say wasn't going to be good news.

"I went to Colorado a few days ago to have the gender surgery, but I love you guys so much I couldn't do it. I feel like I'm dying inside and there's no place to turn."

Nancy with tears running down her cheeks stumbled over her words as she started talking, "This hurts really bad because I feel like I'm dying, too. The future I wanted for us is falling apart and I just don't know what to do or say."

Tears of defeat were now flowing from the eyes of a broken man. He could feel the family life he loved so much slipping away.

"I'm so very sorry. I want to keep trying to make everything good again but I'm so messed up."

"I'll let you stay for a few days because of the kids and see if we can find a way through this but this is the last time. I can't take it anymore."

Dakota stayed for a day then it was extended for a week. Dakota stopped drinking at this point; he was trying everything to overcome the demons in him. He was able to keep himself on track for three months as he remained in Nancy's home in the guest room.

The first of the three distinctive parts of Dakota's life was success at work and he was on track. He was considered a key player on the team that was developing the new luxury division of Japanese automobiles. With still no official name, it was simply called "Project X." The demographic research was going well. Dakota had completed the extensive research on population, income groups, family size and the upward income projections that would determine the target market for the new luxury brand. The target market was identified—BMW buyers, those up-and-coming successful businessmen and women, suburbia-type, single or young marrieds. The design concepts were the result of collaboration among American, Japanese and European designers. First drawn on paper, the concepts were taking shape in clay at a secret studio and approval given to move forward.

Rumor had it that Dakota would become the division vice president for the new brand. Amazing to Dakota, but not so amazing to the people who worked with him. They knew his accomplishments had earned the praise of everyone.

The second distinctive part of Dakota's life, family, was healthy and relatively happy during this time, at least with the kids.

Dakota started the repairing of his relationship with his daughter by replicating the old days, like the times when they enjoyed special dinner dates. On their father-daughter dates they were able set aside everything and focus on their relationship. His early teenage daughter enjoyed everything; she was just that way. Dad felt alive and well when he saw her dressed up, acting like she was dressed for a night out at a Beverly Hills restaurant. She, in turn, felt special and as far her dad was concerned, she truly was. Dakota loved his daughter.

Dakota also loved and enjoyed his son, his "little buddy." They hung out with each other. Even doing the simplest thing was fun, like running around town in Dakota's nice company car, if they did it together. Dakota and his boy got the idea to find a project car they could restore together, just he and his boy, a car that would be his son's on his sixteenth birthday. They located a rundown 1969 Chevrolet Camaro with some fender damage that needed a lot of work. Father and son had no doubt it would be a real looker when it was finished.

The third distinctive part of Dakota's life was the internal turmoil over his gender identity. During this three month time period he enjoyed some serenity. The issue wasn't stirring him up. He wasn't drinking and he didn't think he needed any therapeutic counseling. But Dakota didn't know the significance or the importance of some therapy. He didn't think it was necessary because he wasn't drinking. But he was about to discover that what started at the age of four was difficult to ignore.

The self-prescribed personal restoration project was actually showing great results, at least for the first three months. Dakota got more comfortable talking with his wife Nancy but they both had the gut-wrenching feeling that they were drifting apart. Dakota knew it was his fault. Dakota was building great relationships with his son and daughter but rekindling love for his wife was complicated. The pain he had caused her by his betrayals of her trust would take time to heal. He lived in deep remorse for his past actions, and they both feared that he couldn't maintain what he had started during these three months.

One night, the two of them were sitting outside on the patio.

Nancy spoke first, gently, "Dakota, we knew this was coming. It's here and it's time for me to take care of myself and the kids."

Dakota responded, "Yes, I know. I hate what I have caused you and the kids."

Dakota's voice broke on the last word as he sobbed uncontrollably. He never wanted his marriage to end; that was the worst thing ever. He had been trying so hard for the past three months to save his family life.

Nancy continued with the difficult news, "I just cannot stay in this gender mix-master, fearing every day that you'll run off and change genders. I can't live that way."

Dakota was overwhelmed with sadness. With the tears falling down his cheek and over his lips, Dakota gave up. Deep in his heart, he agreed with Nancy. He felt strongly that he especially needed to protect the kids from his unhealthy gender madness.

"I don't want you to live this way nor should the kids be faced with this crazy stuff. I really want the best for you and the kids, Nancy; I really do."

Dakota felt powerless over his desire to become a female. He felt like a demon had long ago grabbed the steering wheel of his life and driven him to all his gender madness. This force, demon or not, played a radio in his head impressing on him in so many ways, day after day, situation after situation, that he was a female. The persistent repetition had gone on for too many years. It derailed his ability to keep control of his thoughts.

Dakota's life of forty years had been built on secrets, shame and sorrow. Dakota kept secrets and the kind of secrets he was keeping filled him with shame and sorrow. He felt shame because although he had a desire to stop doing something that seemed so wrong, he couldn't. He felt shame because, if he was truly being honest with himself, he knew that at times he enjoyed the seductive lure of changing genders. He felt sorrow because by keeping the terrible nature of those thoughts from his wife, he was killing his marriage.

Dakota could feel himself falling apart. Broken. His marriage was in shambles; no, it was over. His hopes for family life were gone. He couldn't help but notice the contrast between being a superstar at work and such an absolute failure at everything else.

Dakota was tired of hiding the truth from his wife. Dakota really wanted to stop holding on to the secrets. Sitting there with Nancy, Dakota finally opened up.

"Nancy, there is something I need to tell you. Many months ago I went to see a gender specialist in San Francisco and he diagnosed me with a condition called gender dysphoria."

Nancy was furious because she knew this was just more piece of bad news she really didn't want to hear. She tried mightily to compose herself.

"What is gender dysphoria?"

Dakota tried to explain, "Basically, it is gender depression. The problem is: the only known treatment is a surgical gender change."

Nancy felt betrayed and her anger showed.

"Damn, you knew this months ago! You went behind my back and then kept it a secret!"

Nancy became convinced right then she no longer could trust Dakota. Something inside of her snapped. She was done.

"Do you think a marriage can survive with all the lies?!"

Dakota knew it couldn't. Oh, how he wished he could turn back the clock and do it over. How he wished he could tell her it wouldn't happen again, but he knew better.

"I don't want to hurt you anymore."

Nancy sharply questioned, "Are those all the secrets or are there more?"

Dakota answered quietly, "That's everything and I'm so sorry."

Nancy stared at the floor and gathered strength for what she was about to say. All the thoughts and feelings she had been processing during this reconciliation time, sharpened by her anger at another betrayal, had solidified into a decision. She looked Dakota in the eyes, "Dakota, our marriage was over a long time ago. I had great hope over the last three months. I wanted our marriage to work and I did see reasons to be optimistic, but I just can't trust you and without trust I can't remain married to you."

Dakota knew he would never be able to restore the lost trust with his wife. He had done far too much damage. That day, he left the home of his wife and kids and moved back to the apartment at the beach near his work and close to the bars.

Back at his beach apartment, Dakota continued working while he walked through an excruciating divorce process. He and his son had completed the build on the project car. The 1969 Chevrolet Camaro looked and sounded great with a 454 cubic inch engine, orange paint and white racing stripes. Dakota held on to it until his son's sixteenth birthday and then gave it to him as a gift.

After several months the divorce became final. With the failure of his marriage, Dakota felt battered and beaten down. He had nothing to fight for any longer. The female that had been taunting him for thirty-eight years was winning.

Two years had passed since Dakota's first trip to Colorado to see the surgeon. Would he find a way to overcome the female inside him or would he again, without anyone's knowledge, schedule a trip to Colorado to have the gender change surgery that would give her control of his life?

TEN

The Colorado Trip

The sex change hospital

D akota wanted to make sure nothing had changed the mind of the Ph.D. who had approved him the first time for surgery. So with a phone call, the appointment was made and Dakota, well, it was Nicole, just as before, was at his San Francisco office for her appointment.

Nicole explained to the Ph.D., "I aborted my first trip for surgery. I just wasn't ready and needed more time to process all this."

The Ph.D. smiled and said, "That's a good thing not to rush into such a life-changing procedure." Nicole pressed on, "I wanted to talk to you because now is my time to do the gender change procedure so I can be myself and get on with my life."

The Ph.D. in a tone of approval said, "Nicole I'm very pleased you were willing to come in and review this with me a second time. That tells me a lot about you. I'll prepare a second letter to the surgeon to let him know you've been approved a second time so he'll have no concerns."

Nicole sighed and said, "That sounds good. I'll call and schedule the surgery."

Dakota/Nicole—approved for gender change surgery, two separate times, two years apart. The first approval letter for the surgery was more than two years old but on the second approval letter the ink was still wet. The results were the uncertain part. Would Nicole emerge in Colorado from the body of Dakota?

This trip was much like a replay of the first time: the flight to Denver, the bus ride south, paying the doctor at his office and the walk to the hospital. The second time traveling to this corner of Colorado was easy; Dakota knew the way. There was one important difference this time, however; he was divorced. He was in the depths of hell and despair and the surgery looked look like the only answer. This time there would be no returning to his wife, no dinner dates with his daughter, no project car with his son.

Dakota wasn't going to turn back. He wanted to finally resolve that damn internal conflict. The radical reconstruction surgery would take place as it had been scheduled. At this point, surgery felt a bit like an experiment because no one had any positive proof of success. Was the surgical table not much different than a Las Vegas crap table? If so, what were the odds of success? Dakota would soon experience firsthand the results of becoming the transgender Nicole.

Dakota's lifelong dream was about to become real. All the years of waiting, all the preparation and approvals, all the preliminary feminizing procedures. All the secrets, the drunken nights, the lost dreams of family. All were about to become a memory. The surgery would allow him to turn the page and write a new chapter in his tortured life: a happy chapter as Nicole. Nicole was ready to take her place in life out among the real people. That was her new dream.

Nicole was "snug as a bug in rug" that night, resting in her hospital room, awaiting the early morning surgery. At forty-two years old, long passed were the days with Nana and the dress. Dakota was about to swap genders. His excitement was restrained by the unknown. Now, only a night's sleep divided Dakota from Nicole. Nicole would be the first of two gender change surgeries scheduled that day.

Nicole was wide awake as the nurse came and unlocked the wheels of the hospital bed. The nurse began the slow roll, pushing the bed down the hospital corridors. Nicole, only covered in a bed sheet, was suddenly cold. Was it from fear, adrenalin or the temperature in the corridors?

Nicole asked the nurse who was rolling the bed, "Can I have a blanket? I'm cold."

The nurse replied, "You'll be fine. We're almost there."

Nicole focused on the noise of the wheels rolling across the hard floor. It wasn't yet five a.m. Nicole flashed back to the times under the pepper tree at Nana's, listening to the sounds so many years ago. Even now, focusing on the ambient sounds helped to calm her. Nicole wondered, "Is this Nana's dream come true or a medically necessary treatment?" It was too late now for an answer. The wheels of the bed kept rolling their way toward the surgical room, where the long journey that started at the house behind the wrecking yard had led her.

Dakota had come to believe that the only life open to him was one lived through the eyes of Nicole. He had walked into this Colorado hospital completely convinced gender change surgery was the only possible treatment that could put the end to all the years of pain and confusion, once and for all. The female of Nicole needed to take over the life of Dakota. After living on one hell of a long twisted road, Nicole was taking Dakota down the off ramp to genital dismemberment.

Nicole felt the needle stick in the arm and she entered unconsciousness. Like an artist forming a sculpture out of clay, the surgeon carved away at the male body using a simple surgical knife and, as he declared later on the affidavit, the result of the four hour surgery was the creation of a female.

"Nicole, can you hear me?" Nicole awoke at the sound of the nurse calling her new name and looked up. The surgery was finished. She was back in her hospital room. Nicole felt the afterglow of the anesthesia, floating in a "la-la" land of buoyancy and peace. She felt like the weight of the world had been lifted. The four year-old boy Dakota who stood for the dress fittings at Nana's was now a forty-two year-old transgender in the person of Nicole.

The next day Nicole was recovering in her bed when she was visited by a Catholic nun. The nun routinely visited every patient in the 25-bed hospital. That nun was a simple reminder somehow to Nicole that God was there. Nicole thought the nun's visit was confirmation that God must have given his blessings to having the surgery. Or was it a reminder God would be there to restore another broken life?

Four days after surgery, Nicole was up and about, ready to return to the big world out there as Nicole, a forty-two year-old female. She was discharged from the small hospital and left with instructions for recovery and all necessary medications for the next few weeks. Nicole, not Dakota, stepped out of the hospital in full female attire, hopped aboard that familiar bus for the four-hour ride north to the Denver airport, and boarded the flight that would take her home to start her new life.

Only one friend knew that Dakota had gone to Colorado for the procedure; one friend whom Dakota trusted and who offered Nicole the use of her guest room for the weeks of recovery following surgery. No one else knew; neither his ex-wife nor his employer knew anything about the change yet. Dakota was able to do all that was required for surgical approval, and even undergo the surgery, in complete secrecy.

Dakota did learn how to keep secrets beginning with the big secret at Nana's house at the age of four, but he forgot that holding secrets had consequences.

Strict secrecy meant no pre-surgery counseling was offered to help the ex-wife and kids cope with the radical life changes awaiting them after their father and husband unveiled the new "she." The people closest to him, his family, especially the children, weren't invited to express or process or share their feelings prior to having their lives torn apart by his actions. His ex-wife, Nancy, knew about his struggles, but the kids had no idea. Should they have had a say before a surgeon removed their father from them on the operating table? The gender change would catch them completely off-guard.

Dakota hadn't thought about the impact on his kids. His only concern at the time was relief from the clamor in his head. As a dad, Dakota was devoted to his kids, but his secret surgery could lead others, like his ex-wife, to accuse him of selfishness, possibly smacking of narcissism. How could children blindsided by the news interpret their dad's gender change as anything but a betrayal?

The change from Dakota to Nicole would radically impact all of them, and they would learn about it soon enough. Nicole could be in for some turbulence when that headline splashed across the front page.

When Nicole arrived at the Los Angeles airport, her friend, Marci, was waiting to bring her home and to assist with the recovery. Marci knew Dakota well. They had worked together in the same office for two years and during that time Dakota had described his battle to her. She was fully aware of Dakota's lifelong struggles with gender. Marci had some concerns for Nicole and about her being a success in her new life, but she kept them to herself. Marci was kind and supportive and never told Nicole of her doubts.

Once they arrived at Marci's house, Nicole excused herself. "Marci, I'm going to get some rest. I don't feel well. I have pain in my stomach. I'm sure it's caused by traveling. I just need some rest. I'm going to lie down for a while."

The abdominal pain seemed familiar. It was the same kind of pain Dakota had reported to his general practitioner doctor on many other occasions. The pain persisted over the next several days. It wasn't going away; in fact, it was getting worse. Nicole made a phone call to the doctor who had been Dakota's general practitioner for a long time. Dakota had confided in him about his gender struggles. When the nurse answered, he said, "Hey, this is Dakota. I wonder if I can talk to the doc?"

The nurse replied, "Hold on. I'll see if he can come to the phone." Nicole was on hold for a long time before the nurse returned. "If you can hold on a minute, the doctor will come to the phone."

The doctor's familiar voice was on the line. "Hello, Dakota. How can I help you?"

"Do you remember the abdominal pain I've been having that we talked about?"

"Yes, I do. Is it getting worse?"

Nicole replied, "Yes, it's much worse. It's been getting worse for a week now and I don't know what to do."

The doctor sounded concerned, "Can you come to the hospital where I'm on call today so I can examine you and perform some tests?"

Nicole said, "Hang on, doc. Let me see if I can get a ride there." He turned to Marci, "Marci, can you take me to the hospital in Westlake so my doctor can perform some tests?" Without hesitation, Marci said, "Sure. Let him know it'll take almost two hours to get there in the afternoon traffic. It's about 50 miles away."

Nicole/Dakota told the doc the estimated arrival time as Marci suggested and then added, "Doc, don't be shocked. A week ago, I had the sex change surgery done. I'm now Nicole."

The doctor seemed fine with the news. He said, "Then that's another good reason to see you and make sure all your vital signs are good. Come as soon as you can. I'll be here."

Marci and Nicole gathered their things, got in the car and made the long trip north in the heavy L.A. traffic to the hospital and arrived, as expected, in just under two hours.

Nicole's insurance card from work still showed the name "Dakota." Dakota, however, was looking quite "Nicole" and the intake nurse did a double take. The male name on the card didn't sync with the female appearing person in front of her. But she noticed the note the doc had made about the sex change on the paperwork and finished doing the intake. Nicole was placed into a wheelchair and off she went with a wave to Marci saying, "I'll be done soon and we can go to dinner."

Marci smiled at her friend and replied, "Sounds good to me."

The doctor was quick to schedule some tests and it didn't take but an hour to discover the cause of the pain. Nicole needed to have her gallbladder removed, as soon as possible. The contributing factors weren't fully known, but definitely included too much drinking for too long a time.

The doctor said, "Nicole, your gallbladder needs to come out. I don't like the looks of it. You'll have to remain here in the hospital tonight. I'll make arrangements for surgery to be done tomorrow."

The doctor called Marci to the room where Nicole was and updated her, "There's no need to wait around. It'll be a few days before Nicole will be well enough to ride home."

Unbelievably, Nicole's gallbladder needed to be removed one week and one day after the radical gender surgery had been performed. The surgeon met with her, too, and voiced concern about the lack of recovery time between surgeries but both doctors agreed: the gallbladder needed to be removed right away. The double whammy of surgeries would make recovery tough.

To get the time off from work for the surgery in Colorado, Dakota had taken a two week vacation. Now it was clear it could be three or more weeks before he would be able to return to work. So he called his boss and notified him he was in the hospital for gallbladder surgery. At least that part was true. He told him he would need another week of vacation. His boss said, "No, we'll put you on paid medical leave. Save your vacation time." His swift decision gave Nicole some breathing room around telling the company about the gender surgery. Very convenient.

Surgery went fine. Nicole had tubes running from the nose and the abdominal area into a collection bag strapped to her side; not a very glamorous picture of the new emerging female. She stayed four more days in the hospital and then Marci returned to collect her.

Nicole was very weak. The double surgeries really caused the pounds to drop off and with the loss of weight, a loss in strength. Marci was truly needed now to help the weakened transgender get much needed rest and recovery, and she was eager to pamper her friend. With so little time between surgeries, the newly formed transgender struggled to recover physically. She was in a tailspin because of the horrible shock of two radical surgeries to her body. Weight loss was swift, followed by general weakness and fainting spells. A stomach discharge bag hung on her right side to collect the excess bile that came after gallbladder surgery.

Nicole was under severe mental strain, too. Hiding the truth from everyone she knew, lying about taking a "vacation" to her employer, trying to figure out when and how to come clean with the news were causing her unimaginable stress. When she did tell people, what would be their reaction? How would she deal with the ex-wife, the kids, the boss and the co-workers? Her mind was continually working to come up with plans and examine them from every angle, like turning a Rubik's cube puzzle in various directions to line up the colors on every side. Only this was no game.

The development of the new division of cars didn't stop with Dakota's surgeries and time off to recover. Important media events, previously planned, were coming up and Dakota was front and center on that part of the project. The first was with *Money* magazine. Dakota was to be the company's spokesman in an article about the new trend among Japanese auto companies to develop luxury car divisions.

A week after the gallbladder surgery and one week before the event, Cliff called him, "Dakota, how are you?" Dakota was weak and his voice showed it. "I'm getting better slowly."

Then Cliff dropped a bomb shell. "Dakota, can you return for *Money* magazine night?" he said. "We really need you here. You know how important this kind of event is to the company in assuring we get good press. Talking to you, the one in the very center of project development, is what the magazine writers want. If you could visit with them for about an hour, we sure would appreciate it."

Dakota understood the importance of his being there. No other car company in recent history had launched an entirely separate brand; they were the first. The company was hosting the fun event at a go-kart track, with plenty of food and drink. The combination of play and work with reporters would pay big dividends in how they portrayed the company's new line of cars. The company had a lot riding on the launch of the new division. Heck, Dakota personally had a lot riding on this project. He answered his boss, "Yes, I'll do it. I know where and when it is. You can count on me, Cliff." Cliff's tone of voice in his excited reply let Dakota he had made his boss happy that day.

The night of the *Money* magazine event, Dakota was there, performing his duties one-hundred percent for the company. Marci had driven him there. No one knew about the gender surgery, of course. Dakota didn't show up in his new persona, Nicole, but as Dakota, the one everyone knew and expected. Not many knew about the emergency gallbladder surgery and some looked at Dakota in shock to see him moving like an old man. He was visibly suffering, bent over, moving slowly in some pain.

Dakota was in a world of hurt but, as usual, performed flawlessly with a smile under extreme personal conditions. The company was highly complimentary of his efforts that night and the article that came later was outstanding. The company brass loved it but then Dakota was counted among the brass at that time.

Nicole spent over a month at Marci's recovering. Marci made all the difference in her recovery. But even in her support of the gender transition Marci had her own concerns about the gender surgery but she didn't tell Nicole until much later.

Desperately trying to make life normal, and still not figuring out when and how to divulge his new identity at work, Dakota returned to his job as Dakota, not Nicole. At work, Dakota picked up where he left off as if nothing was any different. "Dakota" remained the identity of the employee who showed up at work, while "Nicole" was the identity of the one who lived in a rented room in an expensive house with nice water views.

Nicole was definitely a novelty to her three roommates who didn't care a bit about her gender. One of the renters used the house as a base for his personal cocaine distribution business. The buyers of the illicit drug included police officers, bank loan officers, a jewelry store owner and many other businessmen in the community. The drug seller and his customers routinely met in the living room and "tested the product."

Time passed and Nicole kept her female identity secret from the company. It wasn't official yet, anyway. The affidavit signed by the surgeon authorizing the change in gender first needed to go through the California court system. Using the legal affidavit as evidence of gender change, Nicole could petition the court to legally change name and gender on the original birth record. The forty-two year-old man named Dakota could be effectively erased from his birth certificate as if he had never existed and a different person, a woman named Nicole, would emerge, quite alive.

Nicole contacted a lawyer to start the process, and after he submitted her request, he insisted that Nicole notify her employer of the upcoming legal change in gender, being that the petition was working its way through the court system and would be approved soon.

Nicole was concerned about notifying the company and with good reason. In 1983, few gender changers were known and corporate support for those who changed genders simply didn't exist. What would be the response from a major Japanese corporation when it was faced for the first time with a high-ranking employee changing his gender to female? Would it be negative, positive, or neutral? The odds were definitely not in Nicole's favor, but she had such good rapport with everyone, she hoped for the best. She reasoned that they probably wouldn't let her continue in a high-visibility role, like the one she had, but she would be an asset in plenty of other positions behind the scenes, out of view.

Dakota prepared himself mentally to drop the gender change bomb. One day in October, he went to the assistant vice president of human resources who reported to Cliff and dealt with employee issues. With a few simple words, Dakota let the company in on his tightly-held secret: "I want you to know I have undergone a surgical gender change. In the weeks to come my name will be changed legally from Dakota to Nicole. I want the company to assist me in this important change."

Cliff's guy responded like the professional he was, "This must be difficult for you." Then he told Dakota: "The company HR department will review the change. The review process will consider how this will impact other staff and how it will impact the important contacts you have with outside companies, such as the national research firm." Dakota nodded and said, "Yes, I can see that. It's understandable from the company's perspective to review the impact."

Within ninety minutes of Dakota's notification to the company, the same professional, the head of human resources, came to Dakota and dropped his own bomb on Dakota with some strong words. "You will not return to your job today," he said. "We'll contact you in a few days after we've completed our review of your job and the impact your identity change will have on the company. In the meantime, remain at home and don't come to the campus." Dakota got a sinking feeling in his gut from the way the response was delivered that his career could be done, finished, over. No gold watch, no going away party. The end.

About three days later, the head of HR called and said, "Tomorrow, at 11:30, go to the Premiere Steakhouse in Long

Beach. Someone will be meeting you to have lunch and discuss the change of name and gender. Plan to spend about an hour and a half going over paperwork and details." Nicole couldn't tell what was going to happen. She felt both hopeful and anxious. Another big step in the transition from Dakota to Nicole would be complete after this lunch.

At the appointed time, Nicole, looking her best, entered the door of the steakhouse. Much to her surprise, standing there was her direct boss, the head of product planning and development, Tom. After some awkward hellos, they were shown to a table. Tom pulled out some papers. "Probably the paperwork to change my name," Nicole thought.

Tom began speaking. "Here's what the company came up with. We know this is a difficult time and we want to help you because you've served the company well for more than five years. We want to provide you with a new car and five months' of severance pay. In return, you'll sign this document that says you're voluntarily terminating your employment with the company." Nicole was caught off guard. "What if I don't want to sign the papers?" Tom didn't miss a beat. "If you don't agree to sign, you'll be dismissed with no pay because the position you held has been eliminated. If you want, you can fight your dismissal in the courts."

Nicole shrugged and gave Tom a defeated half-smile. After all the years of fighting internally against the female inside, she had no energy to muster a fight against a company which had one of the largest law firms in L.A. representing them. "Okay," she replied, "Let's get this over with. I'll sign the papers."

Tom said, "Personally, I think this is wrong. But I'm just the messenger."

Nicole asked, "When will I get the car and the check?"

Tom: "They'll contact you tomorrow with the time and location."

The voluntary termination agreement was signed on Dakota's forty-third birthday. Nicole's idea that life would be wonderful after surgery was now in question. She had confidence in her skill and experience, but how easy would it be to find another good position so she could maintain her financial stability?

It was time to share the news with family. First Nicole told his ex-wife about the gender change and asked her not to tell the kids. Next, Nicole told her brother and her mother. The reaction was swift. Each and every family member was horrified. Nancy told their kids. His brother, Danny, disowned him. It was no different than if Dakota/Nicole had tossed a hand grenade in the middle of a family party. Everyone felt like they suffered massive injuries.

Nicole's life started to look more like a crime scene than a wonderful new life. Dakota's gender change ripped away the foundation of the entire family. All were devastated by his action. It tore their hearts out. Nicole could clearly see everything was gone now. Not a dad, not a husband, not a brother and not a son; just a transgender walking away from everyone who loved him. Everyone had their own way of dealing with the loss. For many it was like a death in the family, with anger and grieving to be done by all.

Nicole didn't blame others for their lack of acceptance. In fact, as for the rejection, Nicole thought it was healthy for them to express their rejection. No sense in pretending.

Within a few weeks it was also becoming clear Nicole's future in the automobile industry was also finished. News traveled fast and all the car companies knew of Dakota's gender change. With each interview it was becoming crystal clear that employment in the auto industry wouldn't be a reality. Weeks of discouraging employment interviews turned into months and desperation settled in. The road ahead was looking to be a very rough one, perhaps even more difficult than it was prior to surgery. With her future looking bleaker and more dismal, Nicole turned to drugs and drinking to kill the pain. Paying for drugs depleted the severance pay. With no savings and no job, she was homeless for the first time, sleeping in a park because she had no place to go.

Waking up in the park, she remembered a friend from several years earlier telling Dakota, "If you ever want to start a program of recovery from alcohol, call me." Nicole got up from the ground, walked across the park to a coffee shop with a pay phone. She paged through the battered and torn phone directory that hung from a chain, looking for the name and phone number of the person she remembered from so long ago. The one who said, "Call me." Nicole wanted to make that call.

Nicole found the name and number. She had no money so she asked a stranger sitting a few feet away, "Sir, would you please help with some change for a phone call?" He flatly refused, "No, I won't help you." But the waitress overheard Nicole's request and she dumped a handful of change in front of Nicole and said, "Take what change you need." Nicole thanked her and started sliding the coins in the slot and made "the call."

Nicole's friend, Marilyn, answered. Nicole said, "You told me if I ever needed to start my recovery to call you." The voice on the other end said, "Dakota, is that you?" Nicole replied, "Yes, it is but I'm Nicole now." Marilyn asked, "Where are you? I'll come and pick you up." Marilyn knew right where Nicole was. She came quickly and took Nicole to a friend's house about twenty minutes away. Marilyn had called her friend, telling him, "Kevin, start arranging things at your place. You're going to have a guest who needs to start a recovery program and needs to go to meetings."

That night Nicole walked into her first recovery meeting. Her need for recovery was evident. Usually newcomers at meetings received hugs of welcome, but in Nicole's case, the customary hugs were withheld because Nicole smelled terrible. She wore a matted rabbit fur coat littered with debris from sleeping in the park. But hugs or not, it was a momentous beginning. Nicole's journey to recovery started that clear starlit night high atop a hill overlooking the Pacific Ocean on one side and the bright lights of Los Angeles on the other. Nicole could see the lights of the city in the distance where her early childhood secrets began.

Marilyn's friend, Kevin, became her first sponsor. This guy was an IBM employee with a passion and the finances to assist people in early recovery who needed food and shelter. He provided that and more. Kevin had eight years of recovery himself and his way of "working the program" was to provide transportation to the daily meetings for anyone who needed a ride. This guy had a great sense of humor and was serious about recovery. He enjoyed bantering with Nicole and they became great friends quickly; a good thing for Nicole because she needed a friend.

Every day, her sponsor took Nicole to meetings where people talked about trusting a higher power, admitting they were wrong and turning their lives over to God. It all seemed a little farfetched and difficult to embrace. Nicole knew about God but wasn't sure how to connect with God.

What Nicole did notice when people spoke about their life struggles was that everyone had a difficult past to overcome. The common thread that joined everyone together was their pain and how they abused themselves and turned to alcohol. In the shared experience of pain they helped each other.

The first difficult concept Nicole encountered as a newcomer was admitting she was wrong. It was so much easier to blame everyone else for everything wrong in her life. Nicole preferred to point to Nana, her uncle and others whose actions caused her to do what she did. She didn't want to admit she had made poor choices and taken wrong turns. She didn't want to be responsible for the mess she had made of her kids' lives or her own. That was just too much to ask.

But as she attended meetings, Nicole listened, not to the sounds around her like she did when she was a kid, but to person after person giving testimony about how their lives had been restored to sanity. The stories were amazingly powerful. Nicole was just starting the process that would open her eyes to see the wide wrong turn she had made that destroyed her life. More importantly, she would discover the turn that could bring her back home.

Nicole's heart was opening to understanding. She admitted she was wrong and that she was badly broken like "Humpty Dumpty" after his big fall. This was the first gift of recovery. The second gift of recovery was coming to realize that a higher power than herself could put all the broken pieces of "Humpty Dumpty" together again and she could be made new by the higher power of God.

The people Nicole met in the recovery meetings were not religious, not even a little bit, and many beliefs were represented.

But in the meetings, the evidence of God was there. Lives were fully restored, not because people participated in some trappings of religious mumbo-jumbo but because they entered into healthy relationship with God, a relationship that brought restoration. It wasn't complicated, but it would require Nicole to see everything in life in light of her new sober perspective.

ELEVEN

Starting Anew

The pastor who opened his home

Nicole found herself in a situation that was completely different than anything she had ever experienced before. Nicole was being helped and encouraged toward recovery by her new friend and sponsor, Kevin, who was homosexual and she was living in his house with other men in recovery, who were also homosexual. Nicole thought to herself, "This is what you do when you have no place to turn and cannot face your friends and family. You find support from new friends, people you never knew before." It was strange for Nicole because she wasn't homosexual and had never had any homosexual friends. Nicole had concerns that by being around homosexuals she could be mistaken for being that way when she wasn't. Also, Nicole wasn't sure how her new relationship with God would work when she was living with a houseful of gay guys but almost anything looked better than the mess she was in before and sleeping in the park. Living in a home where all the people were in recovery and living life sober was actually fun.

One thing Kevin insisted on was attending recovery meetings. He told Nicole to make it her focus and her only priority. The meetings were attended by every kind of person you can think of, from celebrity television stars to homeless and everything in between. At the meetings, they made it clear that recovery depended on being transparent and honest in everything. Transgenders are routinely rejected by every other social group. But in Nicole's new recovery world, transgenders were accepted as just another person in recovery—nothing special, just an alcoholic in need of recovery.

Nicole followed her sponsor's instruction and attended meetings almost every day. All social events were with others in recovery also. It was a very clean, safe way to start recovery. Then after about one month, Kevin's mother got sick and went into the hospital. Her crazy neighbor noticed her absence and took the opportunity to pour gasoline on her car parked in the driveway and set it on fire. Kevin was concerned that his mother's house would be next. Nicole offered to stay in the house for the few days that Kevin's mother would be gone.

Like many other alcoholics who had entered recovery before her, Nicole felt strong and invincible after only thirty days of recovery meetings. It was about a forty-minute drive from Kevin's house, so Nicole wouldn't have a ride to meetings. It was only for a few days. Besides, Nicole would be about a mile away from people Kevin knew, a Green Beret and a horse trainer who were also in recovery.

Kevin thought Nicole would find the couple's story intriguing. It was intriguing, all right. The two were a heterosexual couple and each had undergone a sex change to the opposite gender. Now the very tall, strong, powerful Green Beret was a woman, and the petite horse trainer was a man, making for a pathetic-looking pair. This couple would prove to be Nicole's undoing.

Unbeknownst to Kevin, the couple was no longer working a program of recovery, but had resumed a lifestyle of drugs and booze. Nicole didn't know at first. The few days of house-sitting turned into weeks as Kevin's mother grew sicker at the hospital. It wasn't until they invited her out for coffee at a bar and she watched as they purchased drugs from the bartender that the shocking truth of their deception hit her.

The ugly flipside of recovery from alcohol, called relapse, came quickly to Nicole. She had one drink, then two, and so on. She ended up on the floor of her nice temporary home vomiting blood and making a call to 911 for a necessary trip to the emergency room. Nicole's relapse taught her a valuable lesson: recovery wasn't so easy and disconnecting from recovery support was a bad idea. Relapse amplified the failure that was pulling her life apart.

With a new commitment to make sure her recovery program wasn't derailed by another relapse, Kevin brought Nicole back to his home again, back to attending meetings and being surrounded by sober friends. Nicole wanted to stay sober and learn how to avoid future relapse. Her recent experience demonstrated how fragile and uncertain recovery could be. Going it alone led to failure. Going to meetings regularly surrounded by others in recovery led to a life free from the grip of alcohol. If the testimonies she heard were correct, the way to recovery was to connect with the higher power people always talked about at meetings but never said exactly how to do it. Nicole wasn't sure where God was but she knew it was just too darn easy to take a drink, relapse and end up in the back of a rescue vehicle. She wanted to stick around, listen and learn.

Deep inside Nicole was the man of Dakota, and Nicole knew she needed to summon Dakota's passion for achieving career success and put it towards making her recovery work. It was a new day. Nicole guessed a good start would be to get some counseling to expose and deal with the inner demons. In 1985 transgenders were rare, transgenders who thought they needed recovery were even rarer, and fewer still were counselors who knew anything about helping them. She found one that was willing, but at times, he looked across the room during the counseling session at her, his eyes glazed over and looking confused. How, she wondered, would this guy help her?

Nicole had once been convinced that changing genders would fix everything, but now she was starting to suspect that instead it added another issue and more shame to the pile. Finding work was a challenge. Nicole would try anything, sometimes driving long distances when someone offered her an opportunity. She took odd jobs: making salad and delivering it for a small catering company, being a hostess at a restaurant. Nothing had any longevity.

Nicole looked at the shambles of her life after surgery and had to face the ugly truth: surgery was a complete failure. Surgery was intended to make her life better, but it only made her life worse. Once at the peak of success in her career, now she didn't even have a steady job. She was no longer a loving husband or serving as a model of a good father to the two kids at any level. Her choices and actions hurt not only herself, but the people she loved the most, her children. Facing the truth that her actions harmed her kids cut her like a knife to the heart. The internal turmoil that she thought surgery would banish was still there; she just looked different on the outside. The idea that some surgeon could cut you up and you would be "happy ever after" was looking like pure fantasy to Nicole. She couldn't grasp how everything in her life had gone so bad.

Nicole attended recovery meetings and psychotherapy sessions, trying her hardest to pull life back together. She kept on and stayed sober. The one-on-one counseling gave her a place where she could talk, a way to vent and make some sense out of her present situation. To Nicole, who was trying so hard, the consequences of the gender change looked impossible to overcome and she was on an emotional downhill slide. After nearly two years in counseling she was still distraught over all the loss, discouraged and disappointed with her life. The psychotherapy couldn't prevent her from falling into a deep, dark hole of depression. Her gender joy balloon had popped, replaced by hopelessness.

One day, the therapist observed Nicole's growing depression and was concerned she was considering suicide. Talk therapy wasn't covering any new ground. He realized she needed to live in a family setting, with people who would take her in and love her just as she was: a broken, depressed, hopeless, suicidal transgender. He said, "Nicole, I have a friend who, I think, will be willing to help you, to have you come and live with his family in their home for a time, but he lives almost four hundred miles away in the San Francisco Bay area. Would you be willing to go that far for help?"

Nicole was at the end of her rope. She had run out of possibilities. She responded in the only way she could, "I'm open to anything you think will help. I just know I need help." The counselor was relieved. He thought Nicole should know what the family was like so he elaborated, "This family consists of a pastor, his wife who teaches school, a teenage daughter and a teenage son who is in a wheelchair because of a car accident." Nicole thought a bit and said, "This would be very different, but I'm willing to try if they're willing to take me in." The counselor replied: "I'll call them and let you know the answer when you come in next week." Nicole thought it was a long shot and said, "Do you really think your friend would welcome a transgender into his home?" The counselor replied, "We'll know by next week."

All week Nicole considered the prospect of moving in with a family. She was glad she had some time to think it over. The idea of living with a pastor was a bit daunting. Would it be too much religion stuff? Nicole knew the hinge pin to recovery was connecting with a higher power, to her, that meant the hand of God. Coming into relationship with a pastor and his family who knew God was opportunity to find out how to do that.

Would they take her? She had no other options. What else would she do? She held her breath, not daring to hope, as she waited for her appointment time.

The week passed and Nicole was back in the counselor's office. Nicole asked him, "So tell me; what did your friend say about a transgender coming into his home?" The counselor answered, "He wants you to come and join them as soon as possible." Nicole felt like she had won the million dollar lottery. A glimmer of hope broke through her depression. To the delight and amazement of the counselor, Nicole agreed to go north and try living with this family. She asked, "Okay, what's the next step?"

The counselor explained what a great opportunity this would be for her. "Nicole, maintaining your sobriety is so important. With this move you'll be living with a pastor who works in a recovery and treatment center. You'll be able to learn about recovery from a pastor's point of view." Nicole listened to what the counselor was saying, but she thought long-term recovery was just a nice dream. She wasn't so sure it could ever become a reality for her. Her life seemed too messed up. One day at a time was more than enough of a challenge.

Nicole had learned from her own personal encounters with church pastors that they wanted nothing to do with transgenders. Nicole had tried going to a church. The pastor had made a point of telling her, "We don't want your kind in our church," as if he were the gatekeeper for God Himself. Some pastors were too prim and proper ("stuffed shirts," according to Nicole) or too protective of their congregations to allow people like her through the doors. Any transgender was so far out of the norm, pastors shuddered at the idea of a one sitting in "their" church. Some pastors were judgmental, unforgiving, and thought of themselves as better than someone like her. Would this pastor and his family be any different? What was their motivation? Did they have a heart for helping her or were they simply curious to see a transgender up-close?

All Nicole knew about this pastor came from the counselor. The pastor had a Ph.D. in cross-cultural psychology and a master's degree in divinity. He had been the senior pastor of a start-up church. In high school and college, he had been a track star. Nicole's counselor highly recommended him. That was the extent of what Nicole knew of him. Like many other things Nicole had tried in life, this relocation had an uncertain outcome. It could go either way. One positive sign was that the pastor did invite Nicole to come.

Arrangements were agreed upon and the counselor found Nicole a ride with a personal friend who was driving to San Francisco in just a few days. The counselor's friend would drive Nicole all the way to the pastor's home. This experiment in family living could be over quickly. If it fizzled out, then Nicole would have to return to Southern California and try something else.

During the long ride, the counselor's friend said almost nothing so Nicole closed her eyes and slept most of the way. At last, they left the freeway and wound through the streets of a neighborhood. The driver told Nicole, "Here's the address." Nicole could see a long dirt driveway which carved its way for fifty yards up toward an old red farm house almost hidden from view. The only things visible were some old rundown cars that appeared not to have been driven in a long time.

The driver didn't drive up the driveway. He stopped at the entrance on the street, waited for Nicole to hop out, and said, "Good bye." He and his blue Dodge van were gone, and Nicole began walking up the long dirt driveway toward the front door. Her ride was gone; no turning back now.

Nicole knocked on the door. Tap, tap, tap. The door opened and Nicole was looking up at a bald man with straggly longish gray hair growing below the bald top. Nicole thought to herself, "This guy looks like a university professor, not a pastor." The man greeted her warmly and said, "Hello. My name is Matthew, but please call me Matt." Pastor Matt was looking at a transgender woman in a red sweater that fit snugly over her well-endowed, cosmetically enhanced breasts. Bright red lipstick punctuated her lips, her face framed on both sides by long blond hair. Matt reached out his hand to shake Nicole's. She extended her hand, with its long feminine fingernails polished red, and responded, "My name is Nicole." She wondered what Matt thought as he took her hand. Maybe he expected her to have man's hands? She knew her hands looked strong for a woman's. Matt stepped back and opened the door all the way. "Come on in and let me introduce you to my family. We are excited to have you in our home."

Matt brought Nicole inside. There stood Matt's teenage daughter. Like a bell hop, she grabbed Nicole's small luggage bag, telling Nicole, "Come with me. You'll stay in my room. I'll sleep on the couch." Nicole was a little taken aback. She didn't want the daughter to be put out of her room, and protested, "Please, no. I'll sleep on the couch." But the daughter insisted so Nicole would be given the bedroom; that was settled.

The pastor introduced his wife, Mary, and son, Jay, who was sitting in a wheelchair with a smile as wide as the west coast. He seemed like a happy guy. Clearly, everyone looked excited to have Nicole in their home.

Pastor Matt gathered the family and Nicole into a circle and said, "We want to start our time with you in prayer. Because God says it is our faith we rest all our relationships on. I need prayer myself because there are no specific roadmaps to guide us in helping a transgender, only prayer and Christ." He continued,

"We do know it is our responsibility to care for the less fortunate, even love transgenders; scripture is clear about that." Pastor Matt's words were a warm comfort to Nicole. She had never encountered anyone who set about building relationships on prayer and faith. Nicole was instantly at ease and at home.

The first night all five of them sat around and talked. Each family member had their own questions. The environment in this home nurtured the free exchange of information. The family called these times "philosophical discussions." What amazed Nicole was that the family discussions were free from discord even when they didn't agree.

Pastor Matt's wheelchair-bound son, Jay, was always at Nicole's side. Nicole and Jay went everywhere together, two peas in a pod, the most unlikely friends. Jay was almost the same age as Nicole's son. Jay often called Nicole's son to encourage him, letting him know his dad was safe and well. The two of them became friends, too.

Nicole's time with Matt and family quickly extended beyond the initial few days, to a few weeks, then to nine months. Through Pastor Matt and his many contacts and friends, Nicole was invited to meet the owner of a high end retail chocolate store in San Francisco to see about a job. What Nicole didn't know was that the guy at the chocolate shop was the very same one who had given her the ride from Los Angeles to Matt's house. How shocked she was when she entered the store and came face to face with her driver! Even more amazing, the guy became Nicole's boss that day. He gave her a job selling chocolate to retail customers.

Over time, the steady income allowed Nicole to move into her own apartment. She located a small place only about two miles from Pastor Matt's house, with a bus stop directly in front for the bus that could take her to San Francisco. San Francisco wasn't a bad place for someone who was a transgender to be seen working. She had the support and encouragement of Matt and his family, and her boss.

No one was trying to get Nicole to change back to Dakota; not at all. But inside her own thoughts it wasn't long until Dakota started asserting his desire to return and replace Nicole. It was a flip: Dakota was now the radio playing in Nicole's head. The male persona of Dakota wanted to push Nicole out so he could come out and play. Dakota was inside Nicole's head saying, "I'm real and you, Nicole, were fabricated by a surgeon. That's not real." "Nicole, you're the one made in the wrong body." Dakota kept pushing at Nicole that he needed to return to make it all real and now it was Nicole who couldn't fight against it. Dakota's male identity was now living inside Nicole's head. After a few short years of merciful silence, the gender torment had returned.

So, Nicole prepared to tell the owner of the chocolate store that Dakota needed to return as the male.

Nicole looked her boss in the eye and said, "I need to change back to Dakota. I love working here and I want to keep my job with you, but I'd like to change to the male gender of Dakota." Her boss was a bit surprised and said, "Look, Nicole, I wanted to help you so I gave you a job but I don't feel comfortable with you changing genders and then continuing to work here." Nicole replied, "I understand. I don't want to work here if you're uncomfortable with the idea." The boss explained, "The workplace isn't set up for you to work through such issues. It's too much of a distraction to others and to productivity." Nicole responded, "I agree and I completely understand. I'll work two more weeks while you find my replacement."

Nicole went to see Matt after her bus ride home that day. Nicole explained, "Pastor Matt, it's time for Dakota to come back." Pastor Matt said, "That's not necessary. You know we'll support you as Nicole." Nicole tried to explain, "Yes, I know, but I want more to my life than being a surgically-made transgender." Matt counseled her, "I want you to think long and hard about this. Whatever you elect to do, we'll be here to support you and pray for you."

The internal conflict of gender identity with its unresolved twists and turns was causing depression once again. The unfriendly confines of the mind and the turmoil of genders generated enough pain to cause Nicole to relapse before Dakota had a chance to return.

The relapse started in a small downtown biker bar where Nicole threw back a few and then emboldened, tried to pick a fight with a couple of bad-looking bikers. Nicole's behavior prompted the bartender to ask Nicole, "Do you have a friend who can come and get you before you get killed?" Nicole drunkenly answered, "Yes. Matt. His number is 555-1221." The bartender told the bikers, "Back off. Don't hassle this chick anymore." Matt was only about two miles away. He arrived and took Nicole home to be with the family.

The relapse was a major blow to all who were trying so hard to help Nicole. Disappointment was everywhere. Rather than take responsibility, Nicole blamed her higher power. She was in deep gender conflict because the surgery hadn't fixed her. Her blame game was in full bloom.

Pastor Matt thought employment would help. He had a friend who owned a body shop. Maybe working in a man's world would help Dakota "man up." Matt arranged a lunch meeting and the three of them met in a coffee shop. Nicole looked like a girl in men's clothing. JD, the body shop owner, came across like a junkyard pit bull: a tough exterior but inside, he had a soft heart for people like Dakota. JD started the conversation. He turned to Dakota and asked, "So, ya wanta get your hands dirty and come to work in body shop?" Dakota replied, "Yeah, I'll push a broom, run for car parts, anything you want." Matt jumped in, "I think this will really help him but he needs a car to run back and forth." JD said, "No problem. He can drive the shop's diesel Volkswagen pick-up truck as long as he works here." JD, Matt and Dakota settled it quickly. Dakota would go to work in JD's body shop and use his truck to commute.

The plan worked out real well for about thirty days, until Dakota took up drinking again. One morning Dakota started drinking at 4 a.m. and the wheels quickly came off his short-lived recovery. His apartment was only about forty feet from the freight train tracks. Dakota sat drinking in the living room, looking out the window and counting the freight cars as they passed by: one, two, three; and kept on drinking. Driving to the body shop in a company vehicle while intoxicated was a career-ending move. It didn't matter whether Dakota was living as Nicole or Dakota, drinking was a problem for both genders and that needed to change.

Dakota wanted to live as Dakota, a man, but Nicole kept asserting herself whenever he tried. He realized if he was ever to be free of Nicole it would require finding help in resolving his gender issues and excessive use of alcohol. Pastor Matt worked at a recovery facility for prison parolees and was no stranger to the world of recovery. He did some checking to find counselors who also had experience with transgenders. He found one at Stanford University and even arranged an appointment. Strangely, it would be Nicole who would go for the gender counseling because Nicole was the transgender. At least that was the way Dakota looked at it.

Nicole arrived for the appointment on time; unfortunately she was drunk. She politely introduced herself, "Hi, my name is Nicole." The counselor looked curiously at Nicole and asked, "Have you been drinking this morning?" Nicole looked shamefully down toward the floor and answered truthfully, "Sorry. Yes, I have."

The counselor was furious and told Nicole, "Okay, this session is over, but you will sit there in that chair for the entire forty-five minutes and not say one word. Sit there and think about where your life is going." Nicole was stunned. The counselor had dished up some powerful therapeutic medicine in a few short moments.

Nicole sat and listened while the counselor started making phone calls. From the one side of the conversation she could tell the counselor was looking for a recovery home that would take Nicole now. Nicole heard her ask, "Do you have a bed available for a female in your ninety-day recovery program?" Thirty minutes of listening to phone call after phone call felt like ten years to Nicole.

The counselor dialed again and asked the question, listened to the reply, then covered the mouthpiece with her hand. Looking straight at Nicole, she said, "Nicole, this could be your last chance. I have a women's recovery house on the phone and they have one bed available for their ninety-day program. But you must commit right now and go to a detox facility today. The recovery house will take you after you spend forty-eight hours in detox."

Nicole, a little anxiety showing, answered, "Right now? Right this minute I've got to tell you?" The no-nonsense counselor replied firmly, "You'll have a free ride because the home has some funds set aside for scholarships and you qualify." Nicole answered, "Really? It's all paid for?" The counselor told Nicole again, "This could be your last chance. Now is the time, Nicole." Nicole answered, "I get it, but this is so quick." In a split second, she decided. "Okay, I have nothing better to do. Tell them I'll be in the detox facility later this afternoon." The counselors lifted her hand from the mouth piece and relayed the answer, "It's a go. Her name is Nicole."

With this first step, Nicole began her long journey toward recovery. Her turn toward recovery was the result of the cumulative, collective efforts of Pastor Matt's kind concern to find some help, the counselor's tough response, and a recovery home with an open bed and full scholarship. With all the good stuff that came that day, Nicole later wondered if her higher power orchestrated this. She hadn't done anything but show up intoxicated for a counseling session. God seemed to be helping her when she couldn't help herself.

Nicole thought of the numerous "philosophical discussions" she had had with Pastor Matt and the many times he tried to get through her thick skull what faith is and what faith is not, and what being a follower of Christ meant. Over the course of months of conversations, Matt explained his views to Nicole this way: "Being religious isn't necessarily having faith. Religious people all too often put rules in front of faith. For them it is all about what you do and don't do. I don't want to be religious and worry about rules; I want to be a person of faith who has faith in a person, the person of Jesus Christ."

Pastor Matt then continued with his take on the word Christianity, "Christianity is a cultural ideology; not proof the person is a follower Christ. I don't want to be part of a culture; I want to follow Christ."

Finally Matt tried to get through to Nicole another way, "The pivotal point is admitting you need Christ and you need to confess you are living in sin. This pivotal point is where you join in a personal relationship with Jesus Christ. The Holy Spirit will then transform and restore your life." Nicole tried to act like she understood, but the faith stuff was too much for her to grasp. The thought of starting a personal relationship with Christ felt like setting sail into the ocean with no landmarks or charts and relying only on a compass to navigate.

Nicole set her compass toward the recovery home. She desperately wanted to overcome her long difficult journey and this could be her only chance. Crossing the threshold of the recovery home was her acknowledgement that she had made a mess of her life. Nicole was broken. She knew the time had come to turn to away from alcohol and give thanks for the second chance to be restored by God, higher power, or whatever it took; she wanted recovery now.

By staying in the home, Nicole was immersed in recovery life. Fourteen women, under the watchful care of two housemothers, shared the house and all the housekeeping duties. They prepared and ate three square meals together each day. Ph.D. counselors supplied special guidance in groups and one-on-one settings geared toward putting alcoholics on the path to recovery. The Catholic Church ran the home and required all the residents to attend at least one recovery meeting a day. Often the girls were attending as many as three meetings a day. Group events featured speakers who talked about faith and the need for quiet time and prayer.

Slowly Nicole was looking toward the strength of God to fix the mess she was in. The transgender advocates promoted surgery as the treatment and cure based on the premise that God made a mistake. Nicole had gone along with the experts and allowed the surgeons to operate on her genitals as so-called treatment. But in the years after her surgery, Nicole felt differently. She felt God hadn't erred in making her a male. It was Nana's cross-dressing that had given her this overwhelming desire to dress like a girl, even though she was never a girl. The surgery didn't seem to help.

Pastor Matt recommended a church for Nicole near the recovery home. As a transgender who had been rejected by churches in the past, Nicole wasn't thrilled with the idea of trying another church. It was even a bit depressing. Her heart still stung from the time a pastor told her, "We don't want your kind in our church." Nicole did trust Matt, however. If he was recommending the church and its pastor, she might give it a try. Perhaps before attending a Sunday service, she could meet with the pastor at his office to get his views on transgenders and his answer to her pressing question: were transgenders welcome in "his" church?

Nicole scheduled an appointment with Pastor Rob for the next Tuesday. His office wasn't in a church building, but in an old strip mall, and Sunday service took place in a gymnasium at the local grammar school. Nicole noticed that the office was bare budget and no frills. The receptionist smiled warmly and asked, "Are you Nicole?" Nicole nodded and said, "Yes." The lady rose and said, "Well then, Rob is waiting for you." Nicole, a little nervous now, replied, "Wonderful," as the lady opened the door to the pastor's office and a large man came toward them with an outstretched hand and big smile. "I'm Pastor Rob. Pastor Matt told me about you." Nicole said, "Really? You already know about me?" Pastor Rob tried to put her at ease, "Yes, you have quite a story and he told me he really respects you. He wanted me to know how much he supports your recovery journey." Nicole replied, "Yes, if it weren't for Matt I wouldn't be in a recovery home. He is amazing." Rob nodded, "I agree with you about Matt. I'm excited you are here so we can talk. Come on in."

Nicole entered the office and took a seat in one of the guest chairs. Nicole gave him a brief overview of her struggle with gender issues. Then she shared her current struggle with alcohol and that she was in a 90-day recovery program. Pastor Rob was thoroughly involved in the conversation, in the same way that Matt had been when he talked with Nicole. He didn't seem to be judging her or thrown back in his seat by her revelations, in contrast to the pastors she had met before. He leaned forward and assured her, "This church is very supportive of recovery programs and we would be blessed if you would attend here."

Nicole thought that was easy enough for him to say, but what were his real feelings? Nicole pressed him, "Pastor Rob, I have concerns about attending any church. I don't want to be a sideshow or a church experiment where you just want to change me. Will you try to change me back to my male birth gender? Is that why you want me to attend your church?" Pastor Rob, a big man, chuckled as he leaned back in his big chair, "No, we won't try to change you because that's God's job. Nicole, our job is to love you; that's all." Nicole found his remarks, delivered without judgment just love, to be amazing. They talked a bit more and Nicole felt comfortable enough to attend church on a Sunday and see how it went.

When Sunday came along, Nicole got a ride from a gal in the recovery home to the school where church met. Nicole saw a small sign on the big double doors that read "Enter here for church." She sat in the back row, as far away from the people in the front as possible. It wasn't long until a lady came up to Nicole and welcomed her to church, then another lady, then another. Some wanted to sit next to her, too. Nicole was amazed that real women wanted to sit with her, a transgender female. Nicole had no idea if Pastor Rob had told the ladies about her, but all of them were real nice to her. It was comforting. This pastor made his church a place where even a transgender was welcome to come and learn about Jesus and his redemption of broken lives, a place where a transgender was shown acceptance and love.

Nicole wanted her broken life to be transformed and restored. She wondered if recovery and God's love as shown through the people in this church would be enough to guide her to sanity and maybe even spark a bit of faith. The ninety-day mark was coming up, but everyone agreed Nicole needed another thirty days. She was making progress but she wasn't quite ready for life on her own.

TWELVE

The Road to Victory

The recovery home

From the little boy full of life and mischief, wearing torn jeans, a ragamuffin kind of kid just loving life to the transgender female in an alcohol and drug recovery house trying to repair her broken life, Kid Dakota's life showed the effects of the wrong turn taken over forty years ago when Nana secretly dressed him as a girl.

In the mid 1940s, military aircraft filled Kid Dakota's eyes and ears with the sights and sounds of war. President Harry S. Truman, "Give 'Em Hell Harry," took command of this great nation, while Dakota's grandma was trying to take command of a little kid's gender identity with a new dress. Forty-two years later, the sky was no longer filled with WWII military aircraft, unless it was for a vintage aircraft show. The Columbia space shuttle mission flew so high in the sky it couldn't be seen or heard as it orbited the earth. In the mid 1980s, Ronald Reagan was president and no big wars were underway, just skirmishes with Libya and its leader, Muammar al-Qaddafi.

Nicole's ninety-day recovery program extended into four months gave her the confidence that she was ready to start her new life from scratch without dependence on alcohol. The love and support from her church and daily recovery meetings gave her recovery a solid foundation to help her stay sober one day at a time with no other expectations.

Pastor Rob saw changes in Nicole. Her defiance and blaming were slowly being replaced with a new heart in sobriety that no longer looked at the world through shot glasses in dimly lit bars. Pastor Rob knew the Lord had been carrying her all the way to this point. He was reminded of the poem, "Footprints in the Sand," by Mary Stevenson where during the times of her greatest sorrow and need, instead of seeing two sets of footprints, she saw only one. Thinking that Jesus had abandoned her, she asked him why he hadn't been there. His reply: "That's when I carried you." Now Rob thought it was time for Nicole to come to know the one who had carried her.

For Pastor Rob, Nicole's lack of defiance toward the Lord became his inspiration to help her. He knew his job wasn't to judge her but to love her and walk with her until she had that special encounter with Christ. Rob felt he should invite others in his church to provide support for the transgender lady. He personally contacted thirty-five of his church members who would be willing to pray for Nicole and, when it was necessary, to open their wallets to meet her needs. This was love she never thought possible from judgmental "church people." She was amazed.

All Pastor Rob asked in return was for Nicole to write a letter every week explaining her difficulties so the thirty-five would know how to pray for her: prayer for financial needs, housing needs, job needs. Through the weekly letter, Nicole would share her struggles regarding her gender and her recovery. What a powerful expression of love and support. Nicole was astounded that anyone cared about her struggles.

When Nicole found a room in a home with two other ladies, the prayer group helped pay the start-up costs. The group made sure she had money for food. They even provide enough funds for her to purchase a reliable old Honda so she could get to the recovery meetings and to church. This group of prayer people showed with their actions how they truly wanted to be involved in her life and make sure all her needs were met. Their generous support continually amazed her.

Not one person at church ever suggested that Nicole should restore her birth gender, even when she thought she should. They loved on her just the way she was. Their only concern was that she maintain her recovery program.

Completing an in-home recovery program qualified Nicole for special state employment assistance from the California Department of Rehabilitation. The state assigned a job counselor to help Nicole prepare resumes, complete job applications and set interviews. The Department of Rehabilitation would help pay for a wardrobe that was suitable for interviews.

Marilyn Ridge, Nicole's rehab counselor, looked like "Olive Oyl" from the old Popeye cartoon, skinny as a rail with a black ponytail. Nicole and Marilyn got along well, even spending time at lunch together, giving Marilyn an opportunity to learn more about Nicole and her skills, and her life.

Nicole's job search on a scale from one to ten, with one being easy and ten being difficult, even with the power of the state Department of Rehabilitation helping her, was a cool twelve, over the top, difficult. Each interview went well until the interviewer asked the question, "I see you have used another name in your past employment, the male name of Dakota. Tell me about that, Nicole?" Application forms always included a question about other names used. Nicole was truthful and listed Dakota on the application, because the company would find out anyway. The interviewer was aware Nicole was being assisted by the state rehabilitation department, so there was no need for her to hold back. She explained what had happened.

But the truth and the state assigned counselor couldn't kindle even a flicker of hope in gaining Nicole, the transgender, employment. Nicole and the counselor worked together for months, preparing applications and setting appointments for interviews. Nicole had in excess of one hundred job interviews. Nicole was declined every time. Nothing prepared Nicole or the counselor for such devastating results. More astonishing to Ms. Ridge was the reason Nicole wasn't getting a job. It was because she was a transgender and companies weren't willing to employ a transgender. It became clear to the job counselor if Nicole was to have any income it would need to come from the state disability funds. Not because Nicole was disabled, but because being a transgender was a liability that became a disability.

The state arranged for Nicole to be tested for psychological disabilities. If she qualified then she could collect regular disability payments. The tests were grueling, held every day, six hours a day, for three weeks. Many different types of Ph.Ds. probed into her psyche and her skills. The testing of skills included building blocks (yes, small wooden blocks), spelling, math and writing. The psychological tests consisted of ink blot, dexterity, psyche evaluations and written tests. It was as humiliating as it was exhausting. The test results were collected and evaluated by a disability board. They concluded that Nicole was suffering from a dissociative personality disorder. She wasn't convinced she had a disorder but she knew the diagnosis would be sufficient to put her on disability.

Nicole, a forty-six year-old transgender, was about to be set aside on disability, destined to a "do nothing" life. No need to go for job interviews anymore. Most likely she would never be able to secure a job again. She hated it. The consequences just keep on falling like dominoes, one strange unexpected, unwanted twist after another. Nicole could only wonder: Dakota was very successful in his career; where did all that go? Was this the end of working? Being placed on disability signaled a turning point that Nicole thought looked more like a dead end than a road to restoration.

Dakota and Nicole were the poster children for when life goes wrong. This disability label caused Nicole to really dislike being a transgender, an unfortunate identity fabricated by a surgeon with a knife who sliced perfectly good body parts in the name of a gender change. Nicole's body was manufactured from the Kid Dakota, a boy whose young mind was forever changed at his grandma's house.

Nicole was no quitter. She would just have to continue to build relationships in the church and to stay sober by going to meetings and learning from her two sponsors. She wasn't willing to give up on life and let the state determine her destiny. Nicole was ready to get out of the mess she had made. It was time to make good things happen and get beyond the transgender life. She decided she would use the monthly disability income to start a new chapter in her life.

Nicole wanted to learn about psychology, behaviors and recovery. She believed something was radically wrong with reshaping a man's genitalia, turning it inside out and then calling it treatment for gender issues. That sounded insane to her now. It was time to crack open some books and learn. Nicole thought she could become a counselor and assist others in their recovery.

Ms. Ridge called Nicole with some surprising news. Nicole's disability status qualified her for a U.S. Postal Service job program: no questions asked; no qualifications needed. The only qualification was to be on mental disability. Nicole could live on this income. Goodbye, disability check. Hello, livable wage.

The church prayer team had ended their financial support a while ago, after Nicole began receiving her disability income, but their prayers for Nicole never stopped. They never gave up on praying for her gender restoration or her recovery from alcohol. Here was a miracle—Nicole, the disabled transgender—had a job!

Things were starting to turn her way. Her new postal job supplied the money to pay the enrollment fee for a two year California counseling certificate program at University of California, Santa Cruz. Nicole would study psychology, pharmacology and the differences between treatment programs.

Over the course of her studies, she would also have internship opportunities in a variety of recovery and counseling settings.

The certificate program started with eight hours of class every Saturday for several months. Nicole surprised herself by getting an "A" grade on every class assignment and always being at the top of her class in grades. The professor pulled Nicole aside one day and said, "Nicole, you need to give yourself permission to get a 'B' or even a 'C' grade on assignments." Nicole replied, "I enjoy digging into the research. I find it so fascinating. I can't help myself." To be at the top of the class was a sign of her commitment. Many of the other students were Ph.D. psychologists, nurse professionals and social workers, all with years of experience who were taking the class as part of their mandatory continuing education. For Nicole, it was personal. Her deep desire was to discover what drives people to want a change of gender that they regret later, and in the process, she might find out what it was in her psyche that drove all those years of compulsively pursuing a treatment that now seemed like insanity.

From time to time in the various classes a professor would be teaching when Nicole would have an "aha" moment. Words in the textbook jumped up at her from the pages. Nicole learned that psychological disorders caused by childhood events often go undetected until later in life. People with unresolved disorders exhibit signs like substance abuse, self-abuse and personality quirks, commonly accompanied with general unhappiness and depression. Nicole grasped that the gender change surgery could never be effective in the treatment of psychological disorders because surgery didn't treat, or even acknowledge, the underlying disorders that could cause the desire to change genders.

This drove Nicole to start trying to bring up memories, everything and anything she could remember from her childhood. Tears ran down her cheeks when she realized she didn't have access to the memories from Dakota's early life. Dakota had his own box of memories that Nicole couldn't penetrate. Nicole had limited knowledge or even feelings that would help her discover Dakota's early life pain. Nonetheless, Nicole wanted answers.

Like an archeologist she tried to unearth the buried memories of Dakota's boyhood. She would sit quietly trying to remember. She could now understand that the surgery was Dakota's way of erasing the memories of his early troubled life by becoming someone else. A change of gender is really a suicide without a graveside service. Wanting to escape his pain, he had discarded his male gender and all the memories as if they had never existed. Nicole saw that, with surgery, Dakota orchestrated his own deathless suicide at age forty-two. Nicole couldn't get to Dakota's memories; only he could do that. She concluded that the only way to get to the memories and heal from them was for her to step aside and restore Dakota to his male gender. Her healing, and his, depended on excavating, exposing and treating the cause of all the pain buried in his memories.

"Changing to Dakota won't be hard to do," thought Nicole. "The surgery never changed my gender in the first place. The elaborate cosmetic procedures changed my appearance so I could successfully present myself as female, but after living as a female, now I know it was only an effective masquerade, not a gender change." Nicole's psychology studies made it clear that a person changing genders was like an actor on a stage dressed up and made up to look like the character, walking and talking the part; just social role playing, not reality.

Nicole could clearly see that Dakota was hiding behind the masquerade so he wouldn't feel the forty years of pain. Sitting late at night alone, a smile came across Nicole's face as she said to herself, "You don't need God to restore your old gender. Just use the brains God gave you to see you have been duped by the flimflam of the gender change." Then she realized what she had said and thought, "Where did that come from?" Maybe the thirty-five prayer warriors praying for Dakota's restoration were having an effect.

Nicole might think that returning to Dakota was as easy as dressing differently, but in the real world, restoring Dakota would be a huge challenge, a real "born again" experience because Dakota's official life had been purged from all the records. Kid Dakota was gone; his eradication was complete. Dakota no longer had a birth record. His name was removed from the birth record, Social Security card, driver's license, medical records, and bank records. According to the annals of history, Kid Dakota never existed. How to de-transition and restore one's male gender wasn't shown on a roadmap or available in a book called "Reversing Your Sex Change for Dummies." It was going to be a learn-as-you-go experience. But for Nicole the light was on: the whole damn gender change idea was crazy.

Nicole found that going back from female to male took time. Physical changes to the body aren't undone by a simple snap of the fingers. Getting off female hormones took some delicate maneuvering. Hormones are nothing to casually mess with. Removing the breast implants was a surgical procedure and Nicole's arm movement was restricted while she healed. That brought problems for Nicole's third shift job at the Postal Service. She couldn't lift the mail bins. Nicole wasn't a permanent employee, so she didn't have paid leave. They told her to quit and go find something else.

Nicole decided to see Ms. Ridge at the State Department of Rehabilitation. That's when she discovered the state wanted to give up on her because changing back to Dakota was crazy. The state wanted her to undergo even more testing to evaluate if the state would continue to help her find a job. Nicole underwent tests for several weeks, not so much psychological but for evaluated her skills. When the tests showed that she had a ninth grade reading ability and difficulties with memory loss, the state concluded this made it impossible for her to work and therefore, the state was off the hook to help her find a job. Without any fanfare her disability status was elevated to permanent disability, based on the dissociative personality disorder suggested by the first set of tests and the low skills demonstrated on the latest ones. Over Nicole's objections, the state filed papers declaring that she was permanently disabled.

The word recovery took on a much bigger meaning—it was life recovery now. Like Dakota had a box to stash away his pain, the state placed people like Nicole in a box that contained only pain and no hope for the future. Nicole wasn't as dumb as the tests indicated. She knew there were many steps required to recover from all the stuff. First was to take an extensive personal inventory of her life, of everything psychological she could access. A house cleaning, so to speak. The inventory was to include all the good, the bad and the ugly. The inventory step was often a sticking point for people in recovery programs because people don't want to return to dark places of the past. Most in recovery preferred to stay stuck in denial of the past. It was time for Nicole to complete this step but she wasn't ready yet. Besides, Dakota would need to return for the inventory to be a genuine account from both genders.

By 1989 Nicole had successfully graduated from two university certificate programs that dealt with the psychology of recovery and she had completed three different internships programs. One was an inpatient psyche treatment program. The other two were outpatient counseling treatment programs for substance abuse. Nicole felt she was starting to land on some solid ground. The desire to restore her life meant she needed to openly acknowledge that Dakota was real and Nicole was a female masquerade.

Nicole was now suspecting that the surgery was all a delusional pursuit that had been developed in the mind of a four-year-old boy. She was ready to acknowledge the person of Nicole was only cosmetic to cover up the man underneath it all. She felt strongly that if a surgeon really could change a male to a female, it would have required far more than a surgeon and a knife. Any real change would have required the surgeon to install an all new female reproductive system that could produce a baby, but, of course, the surgeon didn't do that. The surgeon didn't even remove the penis. He simply inverted the male penis turning it inside out to form a female-looking vagina. So, the truth is the penis was never removed.

Nicole became more and more interested in the writings of well-known theologians. Nicole was browsing the stacks in the university library when she came across a poem written by theologian Dietrich Bonhoeffer titled, "Who am I?" Bonhoeffer wrote this poem in May, 1945, from his prison cell one month before he was executed for the crime of speaking out against Hitler's tyranny. Nicole immediately felt a connection to Bonhoeffer's feelings of imprisonment. Bonhoeffer was in prison in 1945 at the very time Nicole/Dakota first felt like a prisoner of Nana's cross-dressing. Nicole, deeply moved by his poem, did her own version of Bonhoeffer's poem to express her feelings. This poem was a reflection of the early stages of her recovery.

Who Am I?

Abuse and fear have carved, shaped and molded this person.
Who am I? It's not clear, or is it fear?
Who am I, the Question asks,
Continuing to scream through the years and tears.
The voice sounds have fallen on deaf ears.
After the tears and fears of all these years
Is it possible to get cheers from our peers?
Have I become an enigma from all the stigma?
It's atrocious to just be known as some diagnosis.
Who am I really—really who am I?

Childhood abuse was just the juice that broke all hell loose;
The juice, like acid, eroded the inner core of Self.
What was the use of that abuse?
Of course ... it must have been my fault.
The pain and anger locked away, like in a vault;
Was all this really my fault?

Listen to my screams this time! Are you listening?
My dreams are lost in the years of screams.
Is that a hand extended toward me? Who is it?

Oh, please reach a little more. I'm here.
I will stretch some toward you. Here's my hand.
Stretch a little more. Grip my hand. Who is there?
Listen to me. I need so much help. Don't let go!
Here is my other hand. Who's there? Don't slip away!

Who am I, broken in so many pieces over half a century,
Fragments scattered across the decades?
Whoever you are, why do you want to help?
Many others turn away; it's too painful for them.
Hey there—guide me, away from the past.
If you open the doors, I know it will be safe to walk through.
There will always be some tears and some fears.
But, whoever I am, whoever I will be, I know
All of mankind is just made up of more, just like you and me.

Nicole had little contact with her kids. She never wanted the kids to be exposed to a dad who wasn't well and acting like a female. To Nicole, forcing young kids to accept the transgender insanity was self-serving and selfish. Why needlessly expose kids to something so psychologically unhealthy when they deserved a healthy father?

Nicole wanted to see Pastor Matthew to explore how he felt about her idea to engage in a reversal of gender, back to male. Nicole also wanted to Matt's help with finding a job in a recovery treatment facility and she wanted to live with him and his family again. She needed the love and support she had always enjoyed in their home.

Nicole drove to Matt's home for this important meeting. She needed one of their philosophical discussions to explore the real life "fork in the road" she was facing. Nicole had questions that needed to be answered.

Nicole: "Matt, I have given a great deal of thought about reversing my gender back to male. I wanted to know: what do you think?"

Matt answered, "That's very difficult to answer. I sure don't want to see you suffer any more than you already have."

Nicole responded, "But more important than suffering is I want to live as a real person, not a person carved by the knife of a surgeon."

Matt in a studied way said, "Look, this is too big of a decision. You don't want to make it casually. I suggest you go back and talk to the counselor who assisted you into the recovery home."

Nicole liked the idea, "You know; that's a great idea. She was a big help to me. I wouldn't be here today if it weren't for her." Nicole was all over that suggestion because it involved some good process.

Nicole continued with more questions for Matt, "I now have the university completion certificates that will allow me to work in a recovery home. What are your suggestions on how to move forward so I can do counseling?"

Matt smiled then explained, "You know; it's possible you could work with me in our recovery program. I'll also ask around for some ideas about other treatment programs."

Nicole said, "That would be great. I have some contacts from my school program but unfortunately they're located too far away."

Nicole continued, "I have one last question. I would love to move back in here with the family if that's possible. At least until I land a good, steady job. What do you think?" Matt shook his head in regret, "We're considering some home construction soon and that will limit the space here." Nicole felt she needed to live with Matt and his family for the support, but understood it wasn't possible, at least now.

Nicole had identified the next step in her process. She called for an appointment with the counselor who had demonstrated tough love and made the phone calls that enabled Nicole's way into the recovery home. If nothing else she wanted to thank the counselor for helping her at such a critical time. It was an exciting prospect, like she was cleaning up the debris of years of poor choices.

When Nicole entered the driveway to the counseling center, she flashed back to the last time she was there: inebriated and overwhelmed with deep emotional pain. This time was very different. A sober Nicole was excited about life again. Walking into the building and down the hallway, and climbing the steps to the second floor allowed Nicole plenty of time to reflect on why she was there today. This counselor was a gender dysphoria specialist who helped people obtain the same gender change surgery Nicole had had years earlier.

Nicole, a bit nervous, entered the waiting room and walked up to the frosted glass hiding the cashier on the other side. Nicole tapped on the glass. It slid to the side and the lady said with a big smile, "Are you Nicole?" Nicole smiled back, "Yes, that's me." The cashier got up and came over to the door to the offices and pointed down the hall directing Nicole where to go, "Third door on the right. The counselor is waiting for you there."

Nicole walked down the hall, the familiar sound of her red flats clicking on the floor. Third door on the right. She opened the door. The counselor got up from her desk and gave Nicole a big hug. With a sigh of relief in her voice, she said, "Nicole! I didn't think you were going to get through the ninety-day program, but I'm glad you did." Nicole with a giant smile of satisfaction, responded, "I wasn't sure myself if I would make it, but that was the best thing I ever did. I really needed to turn that corner and start a recovery program." Nicole went on, "I want to thank you for what you did. It was THE turning point I needed to get into that recovery program."

The counselor beamed and asked, "Tell me, Nicole, why are you here today?" Nicole replied, "Well, now that I have some recovery time and my certificate in substance abuse counseling, I thought it would be a great time to restore my birth gender, reverse my gender back to male. I wanted your advice." The gender specialist counselor look shocked, like she had been hit in the face with a cream pie. Her face turned pink, then red and pink. She said, "Nicole, you are suffering from gender dysphoria. Why would you want to reverse your gender when you always wanted to be a female?"

Nicole reacted sharply, like the counselor hadn't heard her, "If I have gender dysphoria now as a female, like you say, then that means that the gender surgery didn't eliminate the dysphoria I had before surgery. So what was the point of surgery?" The counselor rallied back, "You have the worst case of gender dysphoria I have ever seen." Nicole had thought a long time about this and replied, "You're the expert. Tell me: if surgery was the cure for gender dysphoria, why do I want to restore my male gender identity?" The counselor assured her, "I think you just need to give Nicole more time. You look fantastic as a female. No one would ever know you were ever a male. If you want my advice, I don't support a reversal of gender back to male." Nicole sighed, "Well, I did come here to ask your advice because you have years of experience in dealing with transgenders."

The counselor pressed on, "You really need to give your gender change more time. It has only been five or six years." Nicole wasn't convinced, "If the gender change surgery hasn't worked in five years, what makes you think more time will make it work?" The counselor, "It takes time to adapt to the new gender. Don't do anything rash that could hurt your recovery." Nicole, feeling a little disappointed, replied, "It's been a long time already and I just don't feel real." The counselor concluded, "Just give yourself more time. Stay sober and come back and see me in a few months." With that, the counseling session was over. The two hugged again and Nicole was out the door, not encouraged by the counselor's lack of support for the reversal of genders.

Nicole mulled over what the counselor had said. How was it possible to have gender dysphoria after surgery? All the experts had told her the surgery was the treatment to eliminate the dysphoria. But according to this Stanford University gender dysphoria professional, Nicole still had dysphoria.

Driving home she recalled the day she first was diagnosed with gender dysphoria by the Ph.D. in San Francisco. At the time, she had thought he arrived at the diagnosis rather quickly. Today she couldn't help but compare what happened in her two one-hour sessions with him to what she had learned about psychological diagnosis during her studies and internships at clinics and hospitals. Proper diagnosing of psychological disorders took time, from weeks to months. The process always began with extensive evaluations designed to uncover childhood abuse, trauma or sexual molestations. Then the professionals proposed an effective treatment program, which never included surgery or administering hormones. None of this had happened for Nicole. She had been encouraged along a path of diagnosis and surgical treatment that ran contrary to recommended practice. Now with the benefit of two years of studies, training and internships, Nicole could start to suspect the quackery of the gender experts. To Nicole, a surgical transgender female, it looked like the counselors who approved gender surgery were trafficking in surgery and a grand social gender experiment.

That knowledge didn't help Nicole. She needed much more than that to resolve the deeper issues still causing her gender confusion.

Nicole went back to see Matt and have dinner with him and his family. After dinner, Matt and Nicole went to the living room to talk. Nicole, with great resolve, told Matt, "Matt, I'm going to return to my male gender. I know this is the right thing to do." Matt wasn't afraid to let her know his feelings and said, "I'm not sure about this. I'm concerned such a change could cause you to have a recovery relapse." Nicole had put a lot of thought into it and was eager to explain, "My recovery program is providing the strength and I feel God is in this, encouraging me." Matt shook his head and said, "I don't know if it is right or not, but I'll support you and stand alongside you as Nicole or Dakota." Nicole, with a big smile, replied, "Let's go shopping. I'll need some new clothes so I can start living free of Nicole."

The whole family piled in the car and drove to the shopping mall to support the new Dakota with some new male duds. The family was laughing and enjoying the energy of Dakota's determination. The transition process was unfolding in the selection of new tan pants, nice brown shoes, a shirt, socks and a belt.

The following day Nicole was fading away as Dakota emerged from the barber sporting a new haircut, nice and short so there would be no temptation to go back to being Nicole. He dressed in his new male duds and went to his usual coffee shop. The cashier as usual said to Dakota, "Can I help you, ma'am?" Dakota quickly realized this ride back to his male gender was going to have some speed bumps. Dakota responded to the cashier in the deepest, most manly voice he could, saying, "Yes, I would like a coffee and a bagel." The cashier reacted with embarrassment and answered, "I'm so sorry, sir." Dakota replied, "No problem. It's fine."

Dakota was thoroughly enjoying his freedom from Nicole as he sat in the bagel shop and noticed the eyes on him. He wasn't sure if he was being paranoid or if folks there were puzzled about the male or female persona of Dakota. He enjoyed seeing their confusion and didn't find it troubling at all.

That night Matt came home from the Christian mission and rehab facility where he worked and asked Dakota, "Would you like to come down tomorrow and speak to the leadership about your alcohol recovery as well as your schooling?" Dakota was taken aback and said, "Wow, this is a little scary to talk to Christians." Matt assured him, "There's nothing to be scared about. It's a good opportunity to give Dakota a test run as Dakota." Dakota made up his mind quickly and said, "Let's do it."

The next day at the staff luncheon, Dakota stood in front of a bunch of Christian men, the staff of the street rescue mission and sixty-bed men's recovery center. With his new duds on, fresh and bright, he could be Dakota. He told his recovery story, omitting the sex change stuff, just the alcohol use and abuse and road to recovery. When he was done, applause erupted and each man stood. Dakota felt like a celebrity. They loved his story. Afterward, privately some of the men asked Matt about Dakota's walk with Jesus. Matt just said Dakota was in process.

After lunch Matt went back to work and one of the men gave Dakota a tour of the recovery center. Dakota noticed it was a little rundown, not dangerous, but well-worn. With the tour over, Dakota went back to Matt's office where one of the men Dakota had seen at the lunch meeting was talking to Matt. Dakota remained in the hallway, not wanting to interrupt.

The man stuck his head out the door and waved for Dakota to come inside. He looked at Dakota with a smile and energetically said, "My name is Barry. Thank you for sharing your story with us today. Matt filled us in on the difficult issues of gender that have cost you so much, but which make your journey to recovery even more incredible."

Dakota, a little shy, responded, "You're welcome. Matt and his family have made it possible for me to start and maintain my journey to recovery."

Barry asked a pointed question, "What credit do you give to Jesus?" Dakota squirmed like he had done something wrong and simply said, "I can only speak for myself. Jesus requires a process and I'm still in process." Barry was a little taken aback and said, "That's an honest answer. I respect that." Dakota shared some from his recovery program, "My recovery program requires rigorous honesty so that all I've got: honest answers."

Barry, who was the top dog in the recovery center, looked Dakota squarely in the eyes and shocked Dakota with his next statement. "Our staff came to a quick decision after you spoke today. We want to offer you a part-time, twenty-four hours a week, one-year contract to teach and provide counseling in our recovery program. One great benefit we can offer is your own apartment here at the recovery center for a year at no charge. Think about it and let us know. If you want, you can start next week."

Dakota quickly gave his answer, "Yes, absolutely! I would love the opportunity. Thank you so much. This is a wonderful opportunity to apply my school training in the real world."

Dakota, living now as a man, had just been given a new work situation in which to explore his deep feelings about his gender, in, of all places, a recovery environment. Was this another God thing here? Over the next year, Dakota performed flawlessly all his teaching and counseling duties without a skip back to Nicole. A full year as Dakota! The year had been one of the best ever for Dakota. With great promise, as the one year contract was coming to an end, Dakota had his heart set on a second year contract to keep the good stuff flowing.

THIRTEEN

The Road Back

One step at a time

Dakota's life came with the knowledge of war. World war had raged in Europe and Dakota was in a solitary war of his own. War for Dakota was when teenager Uncle Kyle tortured him with teasing, taunting and molesting many times before Dakota reached ten years of age. Kyle thought he could do anything he wanted to Dakota any time he wanted to do it because he always got away with it.

When Kyle graduated from high school he was encouraged to join the Marine Corps. So, fresh from his graduation ceremony, Kyle was a Marine, thankfully leaving his nephew to live his own teen years free from his uncle's torment. Kyle got into trouble quickly during boot camp. In the early 1950s, he was shipped to the front lines of the war in Korea where he straightened up and became a platoon leader. Kyle wrote letters to the family about the twenty degree below zero freezing temperatures he encountered in Korea. Some of the big battles like the "Devil's Punch Bowl" made the headlines back in Los Angeles. The Korean War ended in 1953 but only after many U.S. men lost their lives. Kyle's platoon was devastated by lost lives but Kyle arrived home safely. He escaped the bullets, but not the psychological effects of battle. The war had wounded him. He drank heavily. He was married five times and never got his life in order. Eventually, his heart gave up from the effects of long-term alcoholism.

Dakota's life was a war all its own. Kid Dakota fought and struggled, waging war on the enemy that inhabited his thoughts. The marching music he loved as a kid inspired him to march on, never giving up on winning his own victory. His battles didn't make the headlines. In his private war, Dakota was fighting an enemy he couldn't see or touch.

Dakota's life was complicated. He felt like he was two people—Dakota and Nicole—co-conspirators in one sense, but in another way, fierce competitors wrestling for total control. He couldn't let either one of them go. And yet he knew that Nicole needed to go in order for him to gain his sanity.

Every day, the two of them engaged in a mental tug-of-war. At times Dakota would get the upper hand, but when his thoughts lingered on what he had done—going through surgery and leaving his wife and kids—he was overwhelmed with horrific shame. Nicole would emerge to give Dakota relief from the pain.

When Nicole was in charge, thoughts of the sham of her masquerade would overtake her. She was persecuted by the reality that no matter how well she was able to dress or do her make-up, she wasn't really a woman. The truth took the wind out of her sails. Deflated, she would take a break and rest from the effort it took to be something she wasn't, and relinquish control to Dakota.

The indication of who was running the show at any given time was obvious with one look at the outer appearance. Nicole preferred to be all dolled up in red lipstick, red pumps and blond hair. Dakota loved dressing in his cowboy hat, belt and boots, all male. Switching between two genders was pure madness; a damn war waged psychologically between Nicole and Dakota. It was a horrible way to live. The urge to change gender and apparel happened spontaneously throughout the day and anywhere: in gas station restrooms, by the side of the road, in a department store dressing room. Yes, Dakota was beaten down. Nicole came back time and time again in an attempt to save Dakota from who-knows-what pain he couldn't face. Dakota wasn't going to live his life in the counterfeit gender madness, but how could he make it stop? He simply wanted to be Kid Dakota again, the filled-with-joy person. He wasn't going to give up. When he doubted, Dakota kept telling himself, "Sure, I'm missing some parts that identify me as a man, but I'm going to have to keep pushing, even if I am a few parts short." It was dark humor, but humor. He still had the ability to make himself and others laugh.

Dakota's one year contract at the street recovery program wasn't renewed, throwing Dakota into limbo on where to live. The apartment in the recovery center was no longer available. He wanted to stay with Matt but Matt's home was undergoing extensive renovation. Dakota was quickly running out of options and out of time. He retreated to the foothills of California to a small gold rush mountain town about three hours away, near one of his recovery sponsors, where he could find a cheap place to live.

For a year, Dakota had been working in the protected environment of the Christian recovery program. People there knew him and his history. They were comfortable with him identifying as a male. But things were different now. Dakota was out there in full public view, wondering if others would accept him as a male. The duality and complexity of Dakota's life made the simplest things difficult.

Dakota had been unable to change his driver's license, social security card and birth certificate from Nicole, female, back to Dakota, male. When Dakota was asked for identification, he turned some heads when he presented a card with the name Nicole. The stares and surprised reactions were uncomfortable to bear. When he moved to the town in the foothills with a fresh start, Dakota felt compelled to assume the identity of Nicole, so that the name and gender on the identity cards matched his physical appearance. He didn't feel like enduring scrutiny, questions and double-takes from potential landlords and other strangers.

Nicole found comfort in the thought of some isolation in the grasslands of the foothills after a year of living among sixty residents at the recovery center. Rentals were hard to come by. The only place available that she could afford was a one room concrete building, six hundred square feet on seven acres. She took it. The acreage provided great privacy while giving easy access to daily recovery meetings a little ways down the hill. Maintaining sobriety was still her number one priority.

The home was like a prison cell, a one-story concrete bunker standing alone in an overgrown field of grass. It didn't take long and Nicole's idealized view of life in the country dropped away. She was all alone. In the deafening silence, Nicole fell to her knees and started weeping in pain at where her life had taken her. She called out, "God, where are you?" with tears running down her cheeks. Again and again she called out, "Help me, please." But no immediate results came, just the same pain and shame that was always there. Nicole, exhausted from yelling and crying, made her way to bed and fell asleep.

Slowly she awoke the next morning, one eye opened as a single shaft of sunlight fell directly upon her face. The light didn't illuminate anything but her face; everything else in the room remained in total darkness. She sensed it was God answering her cries for help. With sleep still in her eyes, she said out loud: "Good morning, Lord," got out of bed and walked to look out the little window. God was shining his sun on Nicole this morning. She didn't feel alone. She smiled and over and over again said, "Thank you, Lord. I see you shining on me. Thank you for listening to my cries." She knew God was letting her know he was there to carry her until she could stand on her own. For now, it was just one set of footprints in the sand.

Every morning thereafter Nicole got up and walked to the window and said, "Hello, Lord. I know you are shining your light on me today and every day. Thank you." She was feeling like her sanity was slowly being restored day by day.

After several weeks in the fresh mountain air, Nicole got a call from Kevin, her sponsor in Los Angeles, who had taken her to her first recovery meeting. Kevin didn't care if she was Dakota or Nicole. Kevin offered Nicole the same room she once had in his large home in L.A. Kevin would take her under his wing again, give her a place to live, and help her maintain her program of recovery. Nicole had had enough of the isolation of that concrete house, even with God's light shining on her. She took Kevin up on his offer. Nicole left the block bunker and headed south to L.A. Nicole had traveled full circle: back to the home where she first started her recovery. It felt good and right, like starting over fresh. Her recovery program was solid.

Within a week after Nicole arrived in the L.A. area, one of the frequent attenders at the recovery meetings, a guy named Corbin, asked her to go to coffee after the recovery meeting. Nicole was always ready to go for coffee. In the course of the conversation, she discovered Corbin was the director of a lockdown psychiatric treatment and recovery program in a large hospital nearby. He offered her a job on the recovery unit as a chemical dependency technician. Nicole was back on the front lines; Dakota had been pushed aside. She jumped at the opportunity to use the psychology skills she learned at university. The pay was outstanding, too.

How strange her resume was becoming with the switching back and forth between identities. Nicole attended university and had the education. Dakota had the experience at the street recovery program, and now Nicole was taking the position in the hospital.

Nicole worked alongside a psychiatric doctor five days a week in the main psychiatric unit. After about two months, he asked to talk with her privately. In brief meetings each day over the next three days, he asked her about her life and childhood.

On the fourth day, the doctor told Nicole, "Nicole, I have been observing you for some time now and after talking with you, I feel strongly you need to be evaluated for treatment of an untreated dissociative disorder." Nicole was shocked and repeated, "You think I have a dissociative disorder? Really? A dissociative disorder?" The doctor replied, "I can't say for sure. Let me give you the names of a few psychologists who can examine your history in detail and then give you their opinion. They are the best of the best in evaluating and diagnosing psychological disorders."

Another pivotal turn in in the life of Nicole had just taken place. Quite by accident, she worked side by side with a doctor who took notice of her behavior and wanted to help her get proper diagnosis and treatment. Nicole was shocked because the only disorder ever considered by the many psychologists she had seen over the years was gender dysphoria. For nearly forty-five years the mystery of Dakota's gender issues had stumped the medical community. Dakota had been plagued with mental anguish for a lifetime and the only treatment ever offered was surgery. The gender experts told Dakota he had gender dysphoria and surgery would fix it. When surgery didn't solve it, the expert told Nicole, "You still have gender dysphoria. Give life as a woman more time."

All of a sudden, Nicole remembered all the testing the state had done when she was declared disabled and unfit to work. The word disorder sounded familiar, but not the term dissociative. Nicole now wondered what the evaluation conducted months ago by the California disability team had found. Was it dissociative disorder? She had assumed it was gender dysphoria. They never gave Nicole the name of the disorder they found nor did they recommend any follow-up treatment for her. They granted her the status of long-term disability, which wasn't effective or compassionate in terms of getting her the help she needed to overcome whatever disorder they concluded she had.

Nicole was appreciative of the doctor taking the time and interest in her, and for sharing his ideas and the names of specialists who could independently confirm his suspicions. She called one of the psychologists on the doctor's list: a lady psychologist with a fancy address in Beverly Hills. Because Nicole worked in a hospital, the lady psychologist made some concessions on her hourly rate. She asked Nicole many questions, all dealing with early childhood experiences. This lady psychologist was looking for answers; Nicole could see that. Nicole knew from her university studies that the psychologist was using the textbook method of patient evaluation.

The line of questioning exposed the cross-dressing, heavy discipline and sexual abuse. After three full counseling sessions the psychologist told Nicole she would take an additional week to write up her evaluation. What would be the outcome? Would she make a definitive diagnosis, or even agree a disorder existed?

The week passed and the time came for Nicole to get the results. She entered the Beverly Hills office building and headed for the elevator. Nicole's life wasn't much different than a trip in the elevator: pushing buttons, riding up and down, and going nowhere. At least this elevator ride landed her on the floor of the psychologist's office. Dressed in the shiny red pumps she loved, Nicole walked into the office. Her curiosity was about to be satisfied.

Legs crossed with a slight bit of knee showing, Nicole sat quietly, comfortable in a leather chair opposite the doctor, a beautiful mahogany desk between them. "One more psychologist to look at this broken down life and give another diagnosis," she thought. The psychologist's eyes were focused on Nicole, a studied expression on her face as she began explaining her findings to Nicole.

"Nicole, it is very evident from my evaluations that you suffer from a dissociative disorder. I feel the onset of the disorder could have been as early as the age of five. Nicole, the gender change surgery you had, unfortunately, wouldn't be effective as treatment."

Nicole felt tears slowly running down her blush-enhanced cheeks.

The psychologist went on. "In fact, the gender change will complicate your recovery from this disorder. You'll have a much more difficult time as a result of your change of gender."

Nicole broke down in tears. Memories belonging to both Dakota and Nicole flooded through her mind: his father's death, the kids who lost their dad, divorce from his wife; all lost in a change of gender that this doctor now said was totally unnecessary. This news devastated Nicole so thoroughly it was difficult for her to take a breath. She thought of all the pain her body had absorbed, cut and ripped apart by the surgeons' knives and now to hear that the surgery hadn't been necessary. How would she even begin to recover from such shattering news? It was beyond her comprehension.

Every fiber of Nicole's being wanted to run away as fast as she could and hide. But she forced herself to get up slowly, walk to the office door, and out into the hallway to the elevator that was truly going down now. Outside on the sidewalk, she walked in her red pumps, the familiar sound of a woman's heel striking the concrete with each and every step. Wilshire Boulevard was filled with the sounds of horns and tires rolling across the pavement. The sounds filling her ears stirred up old memories. Nicole's tears trickled like a leaky faucet. She could see Kid Dakota sitting under that pepper tree at Nana's. The tree couldn't cover and protect young Dakota long ago, and on this day decades later, she was still trying to sort out her life so tortured and twisted by what happened at Nana's house.

Nicole headed toward her car. Walking was helping her to breathe a bit. The reality and implications of the diagnosis were difficult to bear. She felt devastated at the diagnosis and desperately wanted to grab hold of denial. She knew what a dissociative disorder was. It was a psychologically unhealthy reaction to trauma, invented by the mind to escape from reality, evidenced by fragmented identities. Fragmented identities were like alternate personalities housed in the same body. The lady psychologist thought Dakota's identity could have started to splinter as early as five years old.

The diagnosis made sense on some level. Nicole realized Nana had fractured the heart and soul and identity of Kid Dakota, a boy four years old who could be easily molded and manipulated. Dissociating was a way for Dakota to escape the endless pain and deep sorrow. It allowed him to survive as a child, but it wasn't a healthy way to escape. That's also why alcohol, another fleeting reprieve, appealed to him so strongly. Dakota's childhood issues ultimately spilled over into his adult life. His marriage, his kids and family were torn apart because Dakota couldn't ever deal in a healthy way with the trauma of the dress, the discipline and the sexual abuse. Over time, cross-dressing grew into an obsession to assume a new identity in a different gender which the surgeon was happy to accommodate.

The cold reality of what the diagnosis implied hit Nicole hard. She had difficulty absorbing and acknowledging that the surgery, the irreversible gender change surgery, hadn't been necessary and probably would harm her ability to recovery.

The diagnosis of dissociative disorder became the hinge pin to the most profound and pivotal turning point in Nicole and Dakota's life. The fog of the past was lifting enough to get a glimpse at how utterly foolish and reckless gender reassignment surgery was.

Nicole wondered if the San Francisco Ph.D. would have said to her, "You have a dissociative disorder so you can't be approved for a surgical change" that Dakota's life, his kids' lives and his wife's life would have been saved the torment. But the advocate for approving the surgery didn't have a mindset to identify disorders. Dakota had needed a gatekeeper who protected people like him from unnecessary surgery. Instead, he had been put on the fast track to surgery. The approval process for surgery had been quick, like it was no big deal. No penetrating evaluation; no opposition raised. Ever.

And the surgery? What a joke to think it would make a male into a female. Dakota's manhood was still there, no longer outside, but surgically tucked inside. The surgical procedure didn't remove the penis but simply inverted it, outside in. After a genital makeover, Dakota was passed off as a real female.

As far as Nicole was concerned the surgical procedure and gender change now looked to her like a complete fraud. She wondered, "How do they get away with this?"

Nicole eventually came to grips with the diagnosis she had rejected. She was psychologically exhausted but unwilling to give up. Acceptance was the first step. Now it was time to travel another road of recovery, from dissociative disorder to a healthy and productive life. She was ready.

Kevin, the friend who supported Nicole from her very first recovery meeting, and gave her a place to live while she worked at the hospital, was now encouraging Nicole to dig in and do whatever was needed to restore her life fully and get beyond the total madness he had witnessed firsthand. Kevin knew Nicole needed to be near her church family in the San Francisco area. He was supportive and wanted her to find victory in the war of the mind.

Nicole quit her job at the hospital and packed up her 260 Z car to travel north, back up Highway 5 to the San Francisco Bay Area. She was on a mission to replicate the successful alcohol recovery program at the church where Pastor Rob said, "Our job is to love you; it's God's job to change you" and apply the same principles to the dissociative disorder. Nicole wanted to learn about the higher power and how that power could restore her life. She had listened to testimonies where people talked about a higher power providing strength, wisdom and sober living. Nicole now wanted two-stage recovery: alcohol and gender. Nothing was more important now than restoring her life and her sanity. She felt strong but knew she would require therapy to redeem and restore her and Dakota's broken life.

How would Nicole and Dakota's attempt at restoration go this time?

The first order of business was finding a place to live. Pastor Matt's home was under construction, so no room there for Nicole for a few more weeks. A single lady Nicole had known from Pastor Rob's church had told her, "If you ever need a temporary place to stay, call me." The lady knew Nicole was a transgender but was willing to welcome Nicole into her home, at least for a little while. When Nicole called her and explained how she wanted to return to the church and get the therapy she needed for the dissociative disorder, the lady wanted to help Nicole.

Then Nicole contacted Pastor Rob to let him know she would be returning and wanted his support for the recovery she had always desired. The pastor was elated to know she would be attending church with them again. Nicole asked if he had any recommendations for counseling that he thought could help her with the dissociative disorder. The pastor recommended Dr. Cole who attended church there.

Nicole's recovery from alcohol had several years of longevity now. The counseling sessions for the dissociative disorder would be under way soon. More and more, as she attended church Nicole was considering the decision to invite Jesus Christ into her life. But it wasn't easy for her to understand what that looked like. The Bible was big and difficult to read, especially for someone like Nicole who was dyslexic. People told her that joining a Bible study would help. She couldn't imagine sitting face to face in a circle in a Bible study group with all the perfect people. She wasn't one of them.

At the weekly recovery meeting she listened to the stories, person after person sharing their personal paths to redemption and restoration. Nicole knew she need to get real and that meant restoring Dakota to his birth gender but she wondered how to do that.

One step in the twelve-step recovery program was the most difficult and it was often a stumbling block: the personal inventory. Everyone avoided it and put it off because it required admitting all the poor choices you had made and listing all the people you had hurt. Nicole didn't find it easy to admit and confess the surgery had been a very big mistake; hard to openly say, "I was wrong." There was no rush to dig in but Nicole knew if recovery was going to last admitting how wrong she had been needed to come out of her mouth, no matter how painful the admission would be.

Nicole was now asking her psychologist for permission, even support, to go back to work as Dakota. The therapist was concerned about such a move. It was the same old dilemma. The legal documents didn't match the outward appearance. Working as Dakota would require not only an outward gender persona change but also for an employer to overlook the legal gender identity and female name on the driver's license and Social Security card; a real dilemma for any employer.

Pastor Matt learned about Dakota's desire for employment. He approached JD, the owner of the large auto body shop where Dakota had worked previously, to see if he'd be willing to take another chance on Dakota. Matt and Rob both knew JD and thought if anyone would be willing to take a chance on Dakota it was JD. He knew the importance of second chances.

Dakota met Matt and JD at a nice lunch spot near the body shop to talk about the possibility of Dakota's employment. Dakota was back, all decked out in the male duds he got so many months ago. Matt never gave up trying to help Dakota or Nicole; he just kept trying.

Everyone was aware of the risks with Dakota and the potential for failure. But JD was ready to employ Dakota as the shop's parts truck driver. Dakota was looking at himself like he was sixteen again when he worked at another body shop as a parts truck driver. Here he was, starting life over again as a parts truck driver at fifty years old.

Amazing how long the journey and how twisted the pathway littered with broken hearts, broken dreams, a father and a husband, all gone. This day was all about the new road to recovery. Dakota was praying for traction on the slippery road to restoration of his life.

The extra bedroom was finished at Matt's home. Dakota moved from the lady's home to the familiar surroundings of Matt and his family, especially his buddy, Matt's son Jay.

Dakota pushed Nicole aside. His total focus was on being Dakota recovery at every level, but it wasn't easy. His program included weekly psychotherapy, weekly recovery meetings, attending church and listening on Sunday with an open heart to scripture, and working forty hours a week at the body shop. Dakota was learning about the value of healthy relationships that he allowed into his daily life and being receptive to their guidance and accountability to make sure the wheels of recovery remained on the tracks.

Dakota felt it would take courage to leap from just being a good person to a person of faith. He wanted to ask Pastor Matt to take some time to sit somewhere in a quiet place so Matt could explain how that leap of faith was possible. The personal stories at the meetings were so compelling. Faith was looking like the real key that opened that locked door to redemption and restoration. Maybe now was the time to take the leap. Matt set aside some time for Dakota to talk about the transition from being a good person to also walking in faith.

Dakota was never defiant toward Jesus Christ. It just felt like he had done way too much wrong and hurt far too many people to be redeemed and restored to Christ.

Dakota also had questions about the church people who had rejected him. If those were the members of the church, he wasn't sure he wanted in. Dakota asked Matt, "Why do so many churches reject transgenders and not even want them in their church?" Pastor Matt suggested Dakota consider this: "Transgenders represent the secrets hidden within the church leadership. They fear the redeemed transgender because their own lives remain messy and unredeemed." Dakota thought about it and said, "That's amazing. Some churches think they're perfect, but don't realize that they're actually broken, right?" Matt nodded and said, "Correct."

Dakota asked, "If I turn my life over to Christ, how does that work? Matt explained, "Being a good person is very important always, but the key to that leap of faith comes down to a decision: a lifelong commitment to follow the man of Christ. Being a good person is wonderful but that alone will never transform your life." Matt explained, "In a personal relationship with Christ, he fills you with God's power and grace, the Holy Spirit. Transformation and redemption follow from there."

Matt continued to explain the leap to faith, "Invite Jesus into your life, not just to fix things, but to be make you fresh and new, transformed. No longer held hostage by the past. Yes, the past is still there, but it is no longer a roadblock of pain and shame. It is in the rearview mirror."

Matt summed it up for Dakota: "Remember this. Christ isn't a first aid kit. Jesus Christ is a heart change kit. When a good person turns from the desires of the world to the desires of Christ he is transformed and redeemed and receives the heart change."

Dakota listened closely to Matt and took it all in, but he wasn't convinced that Jesus Christ could restore his broken life. Dakota wanted it, but it was just too difficult to believe that through God's redemption a fresh new life was available for the taking.

FOURTEEN

A Relationship that Transforms

Hurts from the past going up in flames

Optimism was starting to take hold of Dakota. Day by day, one day at a time, time went by. Days turned into weeks, then weeks into months and Dakota's life was settling into a comfortable, stable routine. Step by small step, he was learning about faith through prayer and people. The collective impact of his habits—living with a healthy family, working at the body shop, and going to recovery meetings, weekly church services and regular psychotherapy sessions gave reason for Dakota to see a little sunshine on the horizon. Dakota was beginning to feel good in his own skin,

Dakota's skin, and he loved how that felt and fit, the truth of being a man.

Dakota was grateful for the job at the body shop because it meant he wasn't dependent on the government and the Social Security disability program for his income. For Dakota, becoming dependent on the government came with far too many pitfalls. Dakota never felt disabled, no matter what the feds said. Dakota had made a huge mess of his life, no doubt about that. For Dakota there was no giving up. He was determined to restore his life free from the labels of transgender or disabled.

Dakota wasn't the only one with challenges in life. In Dakota's very close group of friends several were themselves struggling. The lady who invited Nicole to stay in her home had been diagnosed with terminal cancer. Another friend from his recovery group committed suicide. Matt's son, Dakota's buddy who was confined to a wheelchair, had received a blood transfusion that was tainted with AIDS. Dakota was deeply aware of how fortunate he was to be alive after all he had done to his body through the years.

Dakota was enjoying working at JD's body shop, and JD saw firsthand how Dakota was making the most of his second chance. That's why, when JD needed someone at a machine shop he owned down the street to make deliveries, he tapped Dakota for the job. The machine shop was a fast-paced environment. Dakota was so speedy at pick-up and deliveries that in just a few days Dakota earned the nickname Rocket Man. The guys in the shop loved the way he hustled all the time. Dakota's days flew by.

In his usual friendly way, Dakota was building relationships among his coworkers. One young guy stood out because he had such a bad attitude. He was always talking trash about himself and others. After Dakota listened to this guy many times, he placed his hand on the guy's shoulder and looked in his eyes and said, "You need Jesus. When you want to invite him into your life, just tell me." The guy looked back at Dakota and said, "Okay, preacher boy. I'll do that." Dakota smiled at him and walked away.

Dakota had been reading scripture every day at work with a couple of other guys. They talked about what they read and how to apply it to everyday events. This small group of guys started eating lunch together and studying the Bible. Dakota thought reading scripture was actually fun, sitting outside around a table in the California sun, eating lunch with the machine shop noise in the background, wheels grinding on steel. Scriptures were reshaping him just like the grinding wheels shaped cold steel. Trying to reshape Dakota's life was no easy task.

Then one day came a big surprise. The guy who was down on himself came up to Dakota with a big smile and said, "I'm ready to have Jesus in my life. I'm tired of feeling down all the time." Dakota was stunned. Dakota wanted a moment to think and said to him, "Let's go outside in the back." They both walked out the shop's back door. Dakota's head was spinning, wondering what would come of the request by a guy who really wanted Jesus in his life.

Dakota spoke first, "So, you want to invite Jesus into your life as your Lord and savior?" The guy answered, "Yes, I do." Dakota looked up to the sky like he was asking for help. He was asking for help, heavenly help. He wasn't sure what to do or say. Dakota prayed, "Heavenly Father, this man wants you to come into his life right now. He needs you. He wants you as his Lord and savior." Dakota turned to the guy and said, "You've expressed your desire for Jesus to come into your life." The guy responded, "Yes, I have." Dakota said, "Then tell him now in your own words." With deep emotion, the guy told God how much he wanted his life to change. Just like that, it was done. Dakota gave the guy a hug and invited the young man to join the lunch bunch for scripture study. The guy gave Dakota a big hug with a nice new smile on his face and told Dakota, "I'll join your lunch group."

Dakota was amazed because he had never before suggested to anyone, "If you want to invite Jesus into your life just tell me." It was completely out of character for Dakota. He felt like the most unlikely guy to bring anyone to Jesus. Pastor Matt had told Dakota many times God uses the most unlikely people to bring people into relationship with Jesus. This must have been one of the times, he thought.

It felt like God was using this guy at the shop to start the transformation process of Dakota's life as well. Dakota remembered Pastor Matt saying to him many times, "God works on both sides of the fence at the same time." He smiled to himself and thought, "Sounds like Matt was right about that. "

Dakota had been working that damn step he had been avoiding, the one required as part of his recovery program that everyone put off doing. The step can best be described as a complete and final removal of all the old garbage. No more blaming others for your broken-down life. For Dakota the time had come to stop blaming Nana, his parents, the abusive uncle. Even the Union St. Ph.D. who approved him for surgery and the surgeon in Colorado who performed it needed to be forgiven and blamed no longer. By doing this step thoroughly and completely, Dakota could make a significant turn from his life of blaming others to one where he accepted responsibility. No longer would Dakota hold on to the resentments and anger, or engage in the blame game.

In excruciating detail Dakota wrote out an itemized list of all the baggage he had been carrying around his entire life. His accounts of resentment and anger toward others were recorded one by one on a yellow-lined note pad. This step was about offering forgiveness to all, every last person, so they could no longer occupy space in Dakota's psyche, a psyche that needed a wall-to-wall cleansing and overhaul. It was time for Dakota to stop blaming his extreme financial difficulties on the companies who refused to hire him. That yellow-lined paper was filling up with old hurts, ugly garbage, unhealthy stuff that took up valuable space in his head. Clearing out the junk would made room in his thought life for love, joy and amazement, the new healthy stuff for his mind.

Then came the hardest part of making the list: confessing the pain he had caused others, especially his kids, by his selfish and self-centered choice to change genders. He acknowledged that he had caused his own kids to suffer pain just as Nana had caused him to suffer. He was no better than Nana. Admitting the unimaginable hurt he had caused his wife and kids was the most difficult part of this step because he had caused them so much suffering. He was no better than all the others. Dakota had listened to recovery testimonials and people always said that forgiving others for what had done to you was so much easier than forgiving yourself for the hurt you caused the ones you love. Dakota was in agony over how deeply he felt about the broken home, broken hearts and broken dreams. It was going to be hard to forgive himself and let go of the shame.

The step required an honest moral inventory: a list of all his defects in character, violations of moral principles, maladjusted and dysfunctional behavior. Well, that was no short list for Dakota, but he kept putting it all down on that ever-growing pile of yellow-lined paper. He kept filling up blank pages: five pages, then ten pages, to twenty pages and beyond. Page after page he listed everything for this mental house cleansing.

The main requirement of this step was to sit with someone he trusted to go over everything he had written on the yellow-lined paper, his personal inventory. Dakota wanted to complete this major step and he knew who he wanted with him: a friend of Matt's, a Christian counselor. The appointment was set for a Saturday when the counselor and Dakota would be the only ones in the building. Dakota drove to the counseling office, a typical commercial building. Dakota held on tight to the yellow-lined paper, all prepared and finished. The step was like a psychological tooth extraction, very painful but required.

This session had no constraints on how long it would last. That was a good thing because the counselor and Dakota were there for nearly three and a half hours. Each item on every page was talked about, painful or not. Everything was opened up and exposed. Many times Dakota's tears flowed as each item was checked off and cleaned up. After the last item on the last page was finished, the Christian counselor suggested they both go into the parking lot and set fire to all the yellow-lined paper. "Let it burn," he said. Dakota nodded and said, "Yes, this is a time for a fresh new start. No baggage from the past allowed."

Dakota had a single match in one hand and the yellow-lined paper in the other. He struck the match. The flame ignited and glowed. Dakota held it to the lower right corner of the yellow paper that contained his writings of that major step in his recovery. The flame transferred from match to paper, and soon the paper was engulfed. Dakota had to let go of the past and let it burn. The smoke and ash from the now blackened paper drifted easily away in a breeze, scattering in all directions. Dakota could feel the past no longer held him hostage. He felt freedom in this fresh start.

The Christian counselor suggested they go back to his office and pray for Dakota's restoration and ongoing recovery. Back in the office they sat across from one another, eyes closed. The counselor began praying for Dakota. After a few moments of listening, Dakota found it difficult to concentrate. His head was down, his eyes tightly closed, his heart open and expectant. That's when Dakota had the most unusual vivid encounter he had ever had. He no longer was aware of the counselor's presence or voice. It was like Dakota was alone. Dakota could clearly see a man descending down from above, coming toward him. He was dressed in a pure white robe. His arms were stretched out as if he was prepared to gather up Dakota into them. Dakota knew he was looking directly into the eyes of Jesus, the Lord. He could feel his embrace. Dakota was in the arms of Jesus Christ.

Dakota was totally amazed. The Lord came unexpectedly during prayer and showered Dakota with a gift that could never be earned. This wasn't a religious encounter. It wasn't a Christian encounter. Dakota never knew how to come into relationship with Jesus. Dakota had wanted to draw near him for a long time, but didn't know how. Somehow, the Lord knew Dakota, drew him close and gave his broken-down, torn-up life an unexpected gift found in the arms of Christ.

The Lord scooped Dakota up into his outstretched arms and spoke so Dakota could hear him, "Now you are safe with me forever." Dakota could see himself in the arms of the Lord. Tears streamed down his cheeks. He knew this was the relationship with Christ everyone had told him about. Dakota knew his troubled life was on its way to redemption and restoration because of this gift.

Dakota opened his eyes and looked at the counselor sitting in front of him. Smiling broadly he said, "The Lord came to me. It was amazing! Jesus stretched out His arms and held me." Dakota shared every detail with his counselor. The counselor had heard of these things happening, but had never experienced anything like that himself. Dakota's encounter with Jesus wasn't a religious experience. Being held in the arms of God didn't make Dakota a Christian either. The encounter was one of the many mysteries of faith that puzzle those who haven't had such an encounter with God.

That powerful personal experience in prayer prompted Dakota to call Pastor Rob. Dakota now wanted to be baptized by Rob and Matt, both men side by side, for his baptism would be a celebration. This baptism would be a public acknowledgment that Dakota had received the only gift that had the power to raise him up from the hell in which he had been living most of his life. Not religion, but the gift of a new life.

It took nearly fifty years for Dakota to be restored to the pure heart of the young boy he once had been. A heart that kept pounding away for that day when Dakota could celebrate victory over his turmoil and trouble. In that brief moment during prayer, Dakota witnessed the Lord reaching out to him, holding him in his arms, and granting victory.

Dakota knew there would be skeptics who would scoff at him for even reporting this encounter with Christ. They would say it was just craziness. Dakota understood why they say that because it cannot be explained. There's nothing anyone could do to earn such a gift; that's why it's called a gift. Difficult to explain the experience, but the restoration that resulted was undeniable. Undeniable because Dakota's life was changed from that day forward.

Epilogue

The power from Dakota's prayer that day many years ago transformed his life. Dakota is now a man redeemed and restored. No more madness, no longer a broken man hiding behind a surgical gender. The evidence of Dakota's transformed life is unmistakable.

What Pastor Rob had said to Nicole, "It's my job to love you; it's the Lord's job to change you," is exactly what happened. For Dakota, his life began to change at the moment when he opened his heart to the Lord.

Dakota knew opening his heart required him to forgive. Yes, Dakota forgave every last person that had harmed him, no matter what they had done. That was the easy part. The hard part was forgiving himself for the hurt and pain he had caused his wife and two children, and many others. Redemption did come to our Kid Dakota. He now lives the life of a man, a husband and father filled with love, no more pain of the past.

Dakota is no longer being held a prisoner of the world view of gender; he is safe in the arms of the Lord.

If you were to ask Dakota: "Are you religious?" he would say, "No. Religion is a bunch of people who are just following a bunch of rules. That's not me."

If you were to ask Dakota: "Are you a Christian?" he would say, "No, I prefer not to identify as a Christian because the word seems to have too broad a meaning today. It doesn't always mean that someone has accepted Jesus Christ as their lord and savior. My beliefs are more specific than that."

Then if you continue to ask, "What would you say about your beliefs then?" Dakota would tell you, "I'm a believer. I believe the Lord is who he says he is because on that special day when I prayed, the Lord came with outstretched arms and my life was transformed."

The old radio in his head has been turned off. No more voice telling him he is a female. Nana is now powerless, gone to her place of rest under a gravestone and her destructive actions no longer hold Dakota's mind hostage. Gone are the days of needing a drink to kill the pain of childhood. Living sober has restored Dakota's everyday sanity. Sobriety started one day at a time, then a month at a time, now several decades of living without alcohol.

Yes, Dakota's life is a testimony as to why we must never give up: not on people, not on God, not on prayer. No matter what comes, no matter how long the journey, we must never give up on the power of God to touch and restore a lost soul.

> You were born an original.
> Don't die a copy.
> -John Mason

More information

More information about this radical treatment procedure can be found at:

www.SexChangeRegret.com

Essential information and stories about sex change regret. Over 100,000 people a year visit the website from around the world and many contact Walt for individual guidance.

www.WaltHeyer.com

Blog of current news and information about sex change regret.

Contact the author

Contact the author at kid.dakota@yahoo.com

More Books by Walt Heyer

Gender, Lies and Suicide
A Whistleblower Speaks Out

Transgenders undergo hormone injections and irreversible surgeries in a desperate effort to feel better, yet they attempt and commit suicide at an alarming rate, even after treatment. Walt digs into the issues behind transgender suicide and shares some heart-wrenching letters from those who regret the decision to change genders.

Paper Genders
Pulling the Mask off the Transgender Phenomenon

A fresh perspective on the medical treatment for gender identity issues, combining well-researched facts with personal accounts. Exposes and debunks the promises of gender change surgery and shines a light on the suicides and dissatisfaction that the advocates would prefer to keep hidden.

"The research, reason, passion (even outrage) and compassion makes for compelling reading."

Perfected With Love
A powerful and inspiring true story

One church says "No" to a scary person. Another church says "Yes" and the astonishing results demonstrate why Scripture says of faith, hope and love that "the greatest of these is love." This inspiring true story will encourage and equip you and your church with ways to show God's love to a transgender person.

A Transgender's Faith

A Transgender's Faith courageously challenges political correctness and the gender change activists who say "Transgenders are born that way" by daring to share the powerful testimony of one man's faith and restoration to his birth gender.

Available at www.SexChangeRegret.com, Amazon.com, and Barnes and Noble.

Printed in Great Britain
by Amazon